He was every bit the rough-and-ready Texas cowboy tonight

Just over six feet tall. Long and lean. Intense and imposing. With a fierce don't-mess-with-me demeanor. He was the kind of man who could stop a heart in midbeat. Or send one racing.

He seemed to be doing both on Kylie right now.

The past three years had obviously been hard on him. She could see the stress etched on his rugged, naturally tanned face and in the depth of his eyes. Stress that she was responsible for.

"Don't make this harder than it already is," Lucas mumbled in a rough whisper.

She knew what he meant. He had to come inside, look around. He'd need to put that on the report. Lucas wouldn't want anyone to question his procedure or accuse him of cutting corners because of the bad blood between them. But he also wanted to do this as quickly as possible so he could get the heck out of there.

Something she totally understood.

SECRET SURROGATE

DELORES FOSSEN

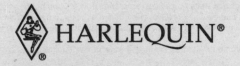
HARLEQUIN®

TORONTO • NEW YORK • LONDON
AMSTERDAM • PARIS • SYDNEY • HAMBURG
STOCKHOLM • ATHENS • TOKYO • MILAN • MADRID
PRAGUE • WARSAW • BUDAPEST • AUCKLAND

For Mickey, Stacy, Selena, Scott,
Trent, Miranda and Hunter

ISBN 0-373-22895-3

SECRET SURROGATE

Copyright © 2006 by Delores Fossen

This edition published by arrangement with Harlequin Books S.A.

www.eHarlequin.com

Printed in U.S.A.

ABOUT THE AUTHOR

Imagine a family tree that includes Texas cowboys, Choctaw and Cherokee Indians, a Louisiana pirate and a Scottish rebel who battled side by side with William Wallace. With ancestors like that, it's easy to understand why Texas author and former air force captain Delores Fossen feels as if she was genetically predisposed to writing romances. Along the way to fulfilling her DNA destiny, Delores married an air force top gun who just happens to be of Viking descent. With all those romantic bases covered, she doesn't have to look too far for inspiration.

Books by Delores Fossen

Don't miss any of our special offers. Write to us at the following address for information on our newest releases.

Harlequin Reader Service
U.S.: 3010 Walden Ave., P.O. Box 1325, Buffalo, NY 14269
Canadian: P.O. Box 609, Fort Erie, Ont. L2A 5X3

CAST OF CHARACTERS

Kylie Monroe—She has no idea that her surrogacy will put hers and Lucas's lives—not to mention their hearts—at risk.

Sheriff Lucas Creed—Since his wife's brutal murder, he's vowed never to love again. But with Kylie carrying his child, he's willing to do whatever it takes to keep her and the baby safe. Now he has to figure out a way to safeguard his heart, as well.

Cordelia Landrum—She blames Kylie for her sister's death, but does Cordelia also want Kylie permanently out of the picture?

Kendrick Windham—The director of the surrogacy clinic who holds Kylie and Lucas responsible for an impending investigation of suspicious business practices.

Dr. Finn McGrath—Lucas's best friend. Or is he?

Isaac Dupont—To keep his unscrupulous activities from coming to light, would this ruthless attorney resort to murdering Kylie, Lucas and their unborn child?

Chapter One

Kylie Monroe tightened her grip on the .357 Magnum and kept her index finger on the trigger.

She waited in the dark. Deep in the corner where she hoped the shadows hid her.

Listening.

Praying.

Mercy, was she ever praying.

Maybe those footsteps that she'd heard outside belonged to one of the deputies from the Fall Creek Sheriff's Office. Heck, she was even hoping it was a neighbor who'd dropped by. Fat chance of that, though. Her nearest neighbor was nearly two miles away, and it was close to midnight. Hardly the time for visitors.

Besides, she'd seen no car lights. No sound of an engine. Or any other indication that whoever was out there had neighborly intentions. The footsteps likely belonged to the shadowy figures she'd seen in the woods on the east side of her property.

She made a quick check of the clock on the mantel. Sweet heaven. Where was the deputy? She'd made that 911 call well over a half hour ago.

Of course, it seemed more like an eternity.

Because her legs were trembling, Kylie leaned against the wall of the tiny foyer and tried not to make a sound. That included humming. Several times, she'd caught herself humming a little louder than was probably safe. Of course, maybe no sound was safe right now.

The baby she carried inside her kicked and squirmed as if he or she knew something was terribly wrong. That didn't surprise her. After all, her entire body was tense—every muscle knotted, her breath thin.

It only got worse when she heard another sound that she'd anticipated.

And dreaded.

There was a sharp groan of wood. No doubt from one of the creaky floorboards on the porch. Someone was just outside her door. Mere inches away.

Her heartbeat began to race out of control, but she tried to stay calm. For the sake of the baby. And for her own sake. So she could respond accordingly.

Unfortunately, *respond accordingly* might mean she'd have to use deadly force.

She was a trained law enforcement officer, Kylie reminded herself. Except she hadn't carried a badge or even held a gun for nearly three years. Maybe she wouldn't even remember her firearms' training. But it didn't matter. She would do whatever it took to protect the baby and herself.

"Kylie?" a man called out. "It's me—Lucas Creed."

Oh, mercy.

That didn't do much to steady her heart rate or her breathing.

However, Kylie did lower her gun, and she eased her finger off the trigger. Sheriff Lucas Creed wasn't exactly the threat her body had prepared itself for.

But he was a threat of a totally different kind.

"I didn't hear you drive up," she informed him.

Lucas didn't answer right away, but she thought she heard him mumble something. A not-so-pleased kind of mumbling. One she understood. Because, after all, her comment probably had seemed like some kind of accusation.

"I parked at the end of the road," he responded. "You told the dispatcher you thought there might be trespassers on your property. I looked around. Didn't see anyone."

That was the good news.

The bad news was that Lucas Creed was standing on her porch.

Kylie eased her gun onto the foyer table and inched closer to the door until her ear was pressed right against it. "I asked the dispatcher to send out a deputy." She tried to keep her voice level. Failed miserably. She had to clear her throat and repeat it so that it was more than an incoherent squeaky grumble.

Another pause. A long one. "One of my deputies is transferring a prisoner to Houston. He won't be back till morning. The other's out sick with the flu. I was the only one on call."

Ah. So that explained it. Lucas had no choice but to respond to her 911. That meant he wasn't any happier about this late-night visit than she was. No surprise there.

He despised her.

Worse, he had a reason to despise her.

"You plan to open the door and tell me what this is all about?" Lucas demanded.

That sent her pulse pounding. If she refused to let him in, it would make him suspicious. If she did comply, the same might happen.

And the one thing she didn't want was Lucas getting suspicious.

"You know the drill," he continued, sounding even more impatient. "I have to do a visual check to make sure you're not being held against your will."

Yes. It was standard procedure. Something Lucas wouldn't violate. Even if she was absolutely the last person on Earth he wanted to see.

Kylie glanced down at her stomach. The darkness hid a lot of things but not the second trimester tummy bulge. Almost frantically, she loosened the tie of her flannel robe and fluffed up the fabric. It helped. Well, hopefully it did. Just in case, though, she angled her body behind the door when she opened it.

And she came face-to-face with a man who'd sworn never to see her again.

"Lucas," she said, her throat closing up.

He didn't acknowledge her greeting and didn't make eye contact with her. Instead, he kept a firm grip on his lethal-looking Glock and swept an equally lethal-looking gaze around the yard.

"Is your porch light working?" he asked.

He didn't say it as if it were a request, either. More like procedure. He had to make sure she wasn't injured. Or that someone wasn't lurking behind her, threatening her. To do that, he needed light.

Kylie reached over, hesitantly, and flicked the light switch on. If she thought it was tough to cope with Lucas in the dark, it was nothing compared to being able to see him.

He was every bit the rough-and-ready Texas cowboy tonight.

Just over six feet tall. Long and lean. Intense and imposing, with a fierce don't-mess-with-me demeanor. He was the kind of man who could stop a heart in mid-beat. Or send one racing.

He seemed to be doing both to her right now.

The past three years had been hard on him. She could see the stress etched on his rugged, naturally tanned face and in the depths of his eyes. Stress that she was responsible for.

Okay. That made her ache. Made her feel guilty. Worse, it made her want to do something to ease what he was going through. She wanted to reach out to him, to tell him how sorry she was. For everything. But Kylie knew Lucas wouldn't appreciate the gesture or the words. And while they might make her feel marginally better, gestures and words wouldn't do anything to help him.

The wind howled, stirring through his slightly-too-long mahogany-brown hair. His firm jaw muscles stirred, too. Moving against each other, as if he were in the middle of a battle about what to say.

Or, more likely, what *not* to say.

"Don't make this any harder than it already is," he mumbled in a rough whisper.

She knew what he meant. He had to come inside, look around. He'd need to put that on the report. Especially *this* report. Lucas wouldn't want anyone to question his procedure or accuse him of cutting corners because of the bad blood between them. But he also wanted to do this as quickly as possible so he could get the heck out of there.

Something she totally understood.

Kylie moved back, still using the door as cover. Lucas didn't say a word. He stepped inside, bringing with him the scents of his well-worn buckskin jacket, the winter frost and the fragrant cedars that he'd no doubt brushed up against to get to her house. His unique scent was there, as well. Something dark and masculine. Something that reminded her that she was a woman.

Oh, no.

That little mental realization shocked her. All right, more than shocked her. It stunned her. Because it had been a long time—years, in fact—since she'd been aware of something like that. This was obviously some by-product of pregnancy hormones. Yes, that had to be it. Because there was no other option. She couldn't be physically attracted to the one man on the planet who would never be attracted to her.

Stupid pregnancy hormones.

They didn't have a clue.

"What happened?" Lucas asked, using his cop's voice to go with the cop's surveillance of her living room and foyer. "Why the 911?"

Kylie quickly tried to gather her thoughts. And not the ones set off by the hormones, either. Those she pushed aside, and she got down to business.

"Around 11:30, I went to the kitchen to get a drink of water." Even though she was trying to hurry this along, she stopped when she heard how shaky her voice was and took a deep breath. This wussiness had to stop. "I looked out the window and saw two men dressed in dark clothes in the woods out near that cluster of hackberries."

He nodded. "I saw the fresh tracks. Could be hunters."

"Could be." And that's what Kylie desperately wanted to believe. That the men were deer or rabbit hunters who'd accidentally strayed onto her property.

Nothing more. "But they weren't carrying flashlights, or if they were, they didn't have them turned on."

Lucas made a throaty sound of contemplation and walked across the living room. His scarred boots echoed softly on the hardwood floor. "It's a full moon. Maybe they didn't need flashlights."

"Maybe, but they weren't carrying hunting rifles, and they ducked out of sight when they spotted me at the window."

While he no doubt processed that, Lucas looked around. At the rough stone fireplace. At her seriously outdated furniture. And at her spartan computer desk tucked between two corner windows. He flexed his eyebrows when he noticed an old-fashioned turntable and the stack of equally old-fashioned Bob Dylan vinyl albums.

Lucas gave a you-still-listen-to-that? grunt and walked on through to the kitchen.

Kylie gave a corresponding yeah-I-do grumble and followed him. She hunched her shoulders, hoping he wouldn't turn that scrutinizing gaze on her.

"Any idea who the two men might have been?" With his back to her, Lucas bracketed his hands on the multi-colored mosaic-tiled counter near the sink, leaned closer to the window and stared out into the darkness. The gesture looked effortless. Casual, even. But she knew differently. Lucas Creed was a dedicated, thorough lawman. He was examining every inch of the woods.

And every word of her account.

"No. I don't know." Kylie shook her head. "I mean, not really. But I had an, uh, appointment in San Antonio late this afternoon. Then, I did some shopping at the mall on the Riverwalk. It was already well past nine o'clock before I started the drive back home, and I thought someone might have followed me. Dark blue car. Nondescript. There was dirt or something on the license plate so I couldn't see it, but I'm pretty sure there were two men inside."

Sheesh. No being a wuss that time. But her story did have a tinge of paranoia to it. His deep male sound of reflection made her think that Lucas might feel the same way. Hopefully, he didn't believe this was some kind of ploy for attention. If she'd been the sort to seek attention—and she wasn't—she wouldn't have been seeking it from him.

"Have you gotten any suspicious phone calls lately?" he asked, moving from the sink to the back door.

"No." She wouldn't tell him about the eerie feeling, though, that something just wasn't right. While she trusted her instincts and intuition, she didn't think Lucas would. He was a man who required proof and facts, and she was seriously short of those.

He turned on the back porch light. While keeping his Glock ready and aimed in his right hand, he opened the door slightly, and eased out a few inches so he could take a look outside. The badge clipped to the waist of his well-worn jeans scraped against the wooden jamb. "You think this might be connected to one of the articles you wrote?"

That improved her posture. Kylie automatically stiffened, and her back went ramrod straight. She hadn't realized that he knew she was a journalist. But then, why wouldn't he? She had a degree in journalism and had worked briefly for a San Antonio newspaper before becoming a deputy. She hadn't exactly kept that a secret.

Unlike other things in her life.

For the past three years since she'd resigned as Lucas's deputy, she'd yet to step foot inside the city limits of Fall Creek, the town she'd once called home. Instead, she'd moved to the tiny country house where her late grandmother had raised her. Added to that self-imposed isolation, she'd been making trips into San Antonio for anything from groceries to doctor's appointments. That minimized her chances of running into Lucas. And it'd worked. She hadn't seen him.

Until tonight.

"The last article I wrote did cause some waves," Kylie admitted.

"Yeah." And Lucas let that simple acknowledgment hum between them for several long moments. "The one about illegal and unethical surrogacy activity."

So, he'd read it. Or at least he was familiar with it. Maybe he was also familiar with the fact that she'd alluded to a powerful San Antonio attorney, Isaac Dupont, and the surrogacy clinic director, Kendrick Windham, who might have participated in those illegal activities.

"I didn't name names," Kylie quickly pointed out.

Why, she didn't know. However, she suddenly felt the need to defend herself and her approach to journalism.

"But along with the San Antonio Police Department, hundreds, if not thousands, of readers figured out that you were referring to Isaac Dupont," Lucas countered just as quickly.

Kylie was sure she blinked. "San Antonio PD? What do you mean?"

He shut the back door and locked it. Then with that same quiet, almost graceful confidence, he strolled toward the laundry room. "On the way over, I made some calls, talked to a friend in SAPD. They might open an investigation based on the info in your article."

The blood rushed to her head, so fast that she became dizzy. Kylie dropped back a step and pressed her hand to her chest. "I didn't know."

"Nothing's official." He didn't even spare her a glance. He continued his investigation by examining the garage just off the laundry room. "Besides, it might not even happen. The police are just looking into it."

She nodded and tried not to show any emotion. But inside that was an entirely different matter. Oh, mercy. She'd speculated that Isaac Dupont might be up to his lily-white neck in illegal activity, but she hadn't thought that article would cause him to try to intimidate her.

If that's what he'd indeed tried to do.

Had he hired those men to follow her? To scare her? If so, it'd worked.

She was scared.

"I'll have another look around outside," Lucas said, coming out of the laundry room. He engaged the lock on the door that blocked off the garage from the rest of the house. "If I see anything suspicious, I'll let you know."

"Thanks." She stepped back, clearing the way so he could go around her. "And thank you for coming."

It was an automatic, polite response. Something drilled into her by her upbringing. A goodbye meant to get him moving out the door.

It didn't have quite the intended effect on Lucas.

He stopped, practically in mid-step, and his gaze slid to hers. Those jaw muscles went to work again, and it seemed as if he'd changed his mind a dozen times about what to say. "This is my job."

A short, efficient, arctic comeback. His version of an automatic response. It was his way of letting her know that even though they were enemies—and sweet heaven, they *were* enemies—he wouldn't lower himself to shirking his duties because of her.

"Yes, this is your job," she acknowledged. "But I don't think anyone in Fall Creek would have criticized you if you hadn't come."

His teeth came together, and the battle began. Not with just his jaw muscles, but with his composure. His eyes. His entire body. "I don't intend to discuss this with you."

No. But it was always there. An unspoken conversation. And it always would be, since he would never be able to forgive her for what she'd done.

But then, she wouldn't be able to forgive herself, either.

That didn't make them even.

She would always owe him. Because of the promise she'd made to a dying woman. Because of the promise she'd made to herself. Kylie would always feel the need to make things right with Lucas.

"If I could undo everything that happened," she said to him, "I would."

He turned. An agile shift of his body. His gaze rifled to hers, a little maneuver that robbed her of what breath she'd managed to recoup. There it was, in the depths of his saddle-brown eyes. The accusations.

The pain.

God, the pain.

Lucas combed his hostile gaze over her face, hardly more than a split-second glance. Then he took that methodical scrutinization lower, to her body.

Kylie trembled.

Waited.

She didn't have to wait too long. Lucas actually did a double take when he noticed her stomach.

Not that it helped, but Kylie adjusted her robe again. Seconds passed slowly, crawling by, until the silence settled uncomfortably around them.

"Are you…" But he obviously couldn't even finish the question. Instead, he swallowed hard.

Since it would be absurd to lie, Kylie had no choice but to admit the obvious. "Yes. I'm pregnant."

He fired a few more of those nervy glances around the house. "I didn't know," he finally said.

The words were void of any emotion. He'd done a better job of that than she ever could have. Because down deep, below the words, even deeper than his eerily calm demeanor, she figured this discovery had to be killing him.

Or maybe he wasn't affected at all because, perhaps, he truly didn't care. Maybe she was a nonentity to him. Nothing more than a 911 call on a frosty January night.

She shook her head, moistened her lips. "Not many people know about the pregnancy." And because she feared other questions, both those spoken aloud and left unsaid, Kylie went on the offensive. "I doubt those men are still out there. But just in case, I'll lock all the doors, keep my weapon nearby. I'll call you if I see anything else suspicious."

He nodded, turned and headed for the door. Lucas didn't even look back, which shot to heck her nonentity theory. She wasn't a nonentity to him, definitely not, because he still hated her.

However, as deep and as potent as that hatred was, Kylie knew that Lucas would hate her even more if he learned the truth—

That the baby she was carrying was *his*.

Chapter Two

Lucas couldn't get out of Kylie's house fast enough. It took every ounce of his willpower not to break into a run, and he was certainly thankful when he made it outside onto the porch.

He immediately pulled in a long, hard breath. Since it was just below freezing and the ice crystals seemed to burn his lungs, it should have cleared his head, as well.

It didn't.

But then, nothing would.

It didn't seem…fair.

There. He'd let the thought fully materialize in his head. Yeah, it was petty. Beyond petty, really. It was spiteful. But it put a rock-hard knot in his gut to know that the woman responsible for the deaths of his wife and unborn child was having a child of her own.

What's wrong with this picture? he wanted to shout to the powers that be.

"Are you okay?" he heard Kylie ask. Definitely not a shout. Practically a whisper.

Lucas laughed. But it wasn't from humor. Damn the irony of this. And damn the flashbacks and the nightmarish memories of that day when his world had come crashing down around him.

"I'm fine," he lied.

"Hmm." She paused. "You know, if I were wearing a BS meter, it'd be going nuts about right now. Because you don't look fine."

He shot her a glance over his shoulder to let her know it wasn't a good time to push this. But then, it was never a good time to push this particular subject.

What he should do was just leave. He should get the heck out of there. Off Kylie's porch. Off her property. Away from her. *Miles away*. Unfortunately, his legs wouldn't cooperate. They'd seemingly turned to dust. So he stood there and pretended to do a routine surveillance of the yard and the surrounding woods.

However, it was anything but routine.

Seeing Kylie again, especially a pregnant Kylie, was like ripping open all the old wounds. Wounds that would never heal. Even though, until tonight, he would have sworn that he was getting on with his life.

And he was.

Well, for the most part.

He would probably never be able to fully recover from the deaths of his wife and unborn baby. Lucas considered that a moment and took out the *probably*. No full recovery for him. He wasn't coming back from that.

But he had a future now. Heck, in four and a half months he'd even get to experience fatherhood. Finally.

No thanks to Kylie.

That thanks belonged to the anonymous surrogate he'd hired through an agency in San Antonio. Only because of her would he get a second chance at having a life.

Hugging her faded blue bathrobe tightly to her body, Kylie stepped out on the frost-scabbed porch. She kept a safe distance, but somehow it still felt too close.

"You're upset because I'm pregnant," she said.

Leave it to Kylie to lay it all out there. That was one of the things he'd always admired about her—her frankness. Oh, and her honesty. Unfortunately, he wasn't in the mood for either tonight.

"How am I supposed to feel?" Lucas replied. And he actually hoped she had the answer. Because he was having a heck of a time sorting it all out.

"Confused. Hurt," she promptly supplied. Her warm breath mixed with the cold air and created a misty haze when she spoke. Against her pale ivory skin, it had an almost otherworldly effect. As if this were all just a dream. He wished to hell it was. "And you're probably mad at yourself for feeling those things since you're not a mean-spirited man."

Lucas scowled. "You're sure about that last part? Because I don't think it's my imagination that I'm feeling a little mean-spirited here."

The scowl obviously didn't put her off. The right

corner of her mouth temporarily lifted before it eased back down.

"Lucas, you're stubborn, inflexible and prone to bouts of misguided stoicism. I blame that last part on your cowboy roots. You can't help yourself." Kylie shook her head, sending a lock of her honey-blond hair slipping onto her forehead. "But you don't have the heart to be mean-spirited."

Probably because it was too close to the truth and because he didn't want this weird intimacy and understanding between them, Lucas decided to end this little personality evaluation. "You have no idea what's in my heart."

"Touché." Kylie waited a moment while the wind howled around them. She shifted her feet. No shoes. Just a pair of grayed weathered socks that were sagging around her ankles. There was a tiny hole just over her right pinkie. "Still, I'm sorry. Being around me like this can't be easy for you."

No.

It never would be.

"The rumor mill in Fall Creek is pretty good," he said, testing the waters. Why, he didn't know. Her pregnancy was none of his business.

And he mentally repeated that to himself.

It didn't help.

He still wanted to know, which made him some kind of sick glutton for punishment.

Her body language changed. Gone was the semi-

cocky demeanor that was part of Kylie's trademark personality, and her shoulders slumped. "I don't think the
rumor mill knew about the baby."

It didn't, or the word would have certainly made it
back to him. He wished it had, and then he wouldn't
have been blindsided by this 911 call. And it was that
911 aspect of this visit that he needed to concentrate on.

Lucas swept his gaze around the woods. Like the
other times, he saw nothing to indicate the hunters, trespassers, or God knows who or what were still around.
Maybe he'd scared them off, and if so, that meant his
job here was done.

Almost.

"Is there someone you can call to stay with you
tonight?" Lucas asked. It was procedure. Something he
would have asked of any woman who'd just been frightened enough to phone the sheriff's office.

"Sure," she said without hesitation.

Now, it was his turn to pause. He angled his head,
stared at her. "If I were wearing a BS meter, it'd be
going nuts about right now. You don't have anyone to
call, do you?"

Her chin came up, but that little display of bravado
didn't quite make it to her slightly narrowed indigo-blue
eyes. "If you mean my baby's father, no. He's not in the
picture. But despite what you think of me, I'm not
totally friendless. I have people who can come over."

However, that didn't mean she would rely on those
people. In fact, he was about a hundred percent certain

that she'd make no such calls tonight. No. Not the independent, my-way-or-no-way Kylie. Once he was gone, she'd lock the doors, turn out the lights and sit there in the darkness. Holding her gun. All night. Terrified. And completely alone.

Hell.

The image of her doing that brought out all kinds of protective instincts in him. After all, she was pregnant. Out in the middle of the woods.

Where anything could go wrong.

"This isn't your problem," Kylie informed him, as if reading his mind. "I'm a big girl. Trust me, I can take care of myself."

"And that's the reason you made the 911 call," Lucas commented.

That earned him another glare. She hiked up her chin again, and she cupped her hands around her mouth. "If anyone is stupid enough to be out there, hear this," she shouted. "I'm freezing my butt off, and I'm in a really pissy mood. I also have a loaded .357 Magnum that I know how to use. My advice? Go home now!"

With that, Kylie turned toward him, making sure that he understood that the *go home now!* suggestion applied to him, as well.

She swiped that lock of hair from her forehead. An angry, indignant swipe. With trembling fingers. Her bottom lip started to tremble, as well. That shot some holes in the steely resolve she was trying to project. It also tested yet more of his protective instincts.

Still, that was his cue to end this visit. After all, she'd practically demanded that he leave, and now that he'd checked off all the squares for this official visit, there was no reason for him to stay.

"I'll be at my house if you need to get in touch with me," Lucas advised. Not exactly standard procedure, but it was a courtesy he would have extended to anyone in his jurisdiction. "Since there's no one at the office, don't call dispatch or 911. Just ring straight through to the house. I can be here in fifteen minutes."

"Thanks." It had a definite *goodbye* kind of tone to it. She turned, her bathrobe swishing like a gunslinger's duster, and went back inside.

Only after she'd closed the door did Lucas realize that at some point he'd stopped breathing. He slowly released the air from his lungs and forced himself to get moving. No easy feat. He felt raw and drained from their encounter.

He stayed on the narrow gravel and dirt road that led from her house to the highway. Walking fast. Trying not to think.

It didn't work.

Not that he thought it would.

The cold darkness closed in around him, smothering him, and with it came the flood of memories. Because he had no choice, he stopped and leaned against a sprawling oak. Thankfully, Kylie's house was no longer in sight, and that meant she wouldn't be able to see him if he disgraced himself by completely falling apart.

And it certainly felt as if that were about to happen.

The adrenaline and the nausea crashed through him. As if the events of that day were happening now, at this moment, and not three years ago. However, three years wasn't nearly enough time to diminish all the brutal details that'd stayed with him. Heck, a million years wouldn't make him forget.

Deputy Kylie Monroe had been on patrol that day when the call came in. A robbery at the convenience store on the edge of town. She'd responded and gone in pursuit of two unidentified armed suspects who were on foot. Even though Kylie had called for backup, she hadn't waited. Instead, she'd begun a dangerous, unauthorized foot chase through the streets of Fall Creek.

That had set off a deadly chain of events.

One of the robbery suspects must have panicked because he stopped and fired at Kylie. He missed. Well, he missed Kylie, anyway. Instead, he'd hit Lucas's pregnant wife, Marissa, who at that moment had stepped out of the grocery store.

The one shot had been fatal.

In the blink of an eye, Kylie had lost her best friend. And Lucas had lost his wife and the baby she had been carrying. Marissa had been only two months pregnant, barely enough time for him to come to terms with the concept of fatherhood. And it'd been snatched away.

Everything had been snatched away.

He'd known that the moment he had rounded the corner and had seen his wife lying on the sidewalk.

Kylie, kneeling next to her. Marissa, nearly lifeless and bleeding, whispering the last words she'd ever say. Not to him. But to Kylie. Marissa hadn't been able to say anything to him because she'd died before he could get to her.

Another irony.

Marissa, the woman he loved, hadn't even been able to say goodbye to him. Yet, the person responsible for her death—Kylie—had been the beneficiary of those final precious seconds of Marissa's life. Her last breath. Her final words. Lucas hadn't heard those words first-hand, but in the minutes following Marissa's death, while Kylie still had his wife's blood on her hands, Kylie had repeated them like a mantra.

Don't let my death kill Lucas, Marissa had told Kylie. *Look after him. Help him heal. Make sure he's happy.*

Make sure he's happy.

Right.

As if that could ever happen. Marissa had used her last breath to ask the impossible. Even if Kylie had ever had a desire to fulfill her best friend's dying wish, he wouldn't have let her try. There was no way he wanted Kylie Monroe to have any part in his healing.

Lucas couldn't bear the pain any longer, so he forced himself to think of his future. His baby. Being a father wasn't a cure-all. It wouldn't rid him of the gaping hole in his heart. But it would get him moving in the right direction. And he couldn't wait for that to begin. Four and a half months, and he'd be able to hold his child.

The sound snapped him out his daydream, and Lucas automatically aimed his weapon and turned in the direction of the noise he'd heard.

A soft rustle of leaves, not made by a stir of wind, either. No. This was much more substantial. As if someone were walking through the woods. But not walking in just any direction.

Directly toward Kylie's house.

That gave him another hefty shot of adrenaline. Not that he needed it. His body had already shifted into combat mode.

Lucas stepped back into the dense underbrush and trees. He started retracing his steps, following the road. Quietly, so that he wouldn't be detected and so that he could listen.

He didn't like what he heard.

Definitely footsteps.

Probably not just one set, either. At least two. Both heavy enough to belong to men. Big men.

And that brought him back to the two possible suspects that Kylie had spotted in the woods.

The trespassing duo had apparently returned for round two. But what did they want? Was this simply a case of trespassing, or was it something more?

Did it have to do with that controversial article she'd written? If so, if they'd been sent there to intimidate her, it could turn ugly. Because he knew that Kylie wouldn't intimidate easily. Even pregnant, she would make a formidable foe.

Lucas eased deeper into the woods as he approached the house. No sign of the men, but the porch light was off again. Maybe because Kylie had also heard them and wanted the shelter of the darkness. If so, that meant she was probably terrified. Worse, she didn't know he was still outside, still keeping watch.

He stopped at a clearing and tried to pick through the sounds and the scents to determine what he was up against. There was a rattle of motion, the sound of a scuffle. Not good. So, he hurried forward, still searching.

He didn't have to search long.

The side door to Kylie's garage flew open. Milky, yellow light speared into the darkness.

So did two armed men. Both were dressed from head to toe in dark clothes and were wearing ski masks.

And they weren't alone.

They were dragging Kylie out of the house.

Chapter Three

Kylie had no time to react.

The two men came at her—fast. Rushing across the kitchen straight toward her.

Her only warning had been the soft click of her laundry room door. That was it. The lone indication that the two masked armed men had somehow picked the lock and had gotten inside her house.

She turned to run to try to get her gun, which she'd left on the table in the foyer.

She didn't get far.

One of them latched onto her, using his beefy hand to stop her. He curved his arm like a vise around her neck. Her throat snapped shut, clamping off all but a shallow scream. But that didn't stop her from reacting.

Her instincts cried out for her to escape. And she tried. She *really* tried. Kylie rammed her elbow into the man's muscled stomach. He staggered back, just slightly, but not nearly enough for her to break free of his fierce grip.

Refusing to give up, she pivoted and went for his eyes using the heel of her hand.

It didn't work.

The man was huge, well over six feet tall and heavily muscled. Literally overpowering her, he grabbed her and shoved her forward into the waiting arms of the other man.

"Remember, don't hurt her or the kid," the first guy snarled. "We're to deliver her safe and sound to the boss. So they can *talk*." His gaze slashed to hers. His frosty gray eyes were the only part of him she could see because he was dressed from head to toe in black, including a ski mask. His partner wore a similar outfit. "Well, unless she gives us no choice about that safe and sound part. I'm sure the boss will understand if she doesn't cooperate."

Terror and a sickening dread quickly replaced the surge of adrenaline. Oh, God.

They might hurt her baby.

She stopped struggling. But they didn't stop. Kylie caught just a glimpse of the white cloth before one of the men shoved it against her face.

Chloroform, maybe.

They were obviously trying to knock her out. But at what cost?

She shoved the cloth away. "You said you wouldn't hurt my baby," she managed to say.

The man put the cloth right back in place, over her nose. "This stuff won't hurt you or the kid," he grumbled. But it wasn't much reassurance coming from a would-be kidnapper.

If that's what he was.

Was this a kidnapping? If so, why did they want her?

Kylie didn't like the first thought that came to mind. Mercy. Was this related to that article she'd written about illegal surrogacy? But it didn't matter if it were about that. If she didn't do something, these men would likely succeed in taking her.

Forcing her breathing to stay shallow so the drug wouldn't incapacitate her, Kylie tried to stay calm. She reminded herself that she had to stay alive and alert for the sake of the baby. It worked. Well, a little. She steadied herself enough so she could glance around the kitchen and laundry room for anything that she could use to escape.

But the men didn't give her a chance to escape. They got her moving outside into the freezing cold night. Away from her weapon. Away from the phone that she'd hoped to use to call Lucas. They hauled her through the garage and out the side door.

Kylie struggled against the drug-laced cloth and managed to bat it away again. But it was already too late. Everything was becoming hazy, slightly out of focus. It probably wouldn't be long before she completely lost consciousness.

She closed her eyes and decided to play along with that scenario. It was a long shot, but if her kidnappers thought she'd passed out, maybe they'd let down their guard long enough for her to escape.

Continuing the act, she let her legs and body go limp and would have fallen if her captor hadn't caught her. As if she weighed nothing, he scooped her up in his arms and kept on walking through the dense woods.

Seconds crawled by.

Each one pounded in cadence with the syrupy pulse drumming in her ears. Kylie fixed the image in her head of Lucas holding his baby, and she used that as motivation to stay awake. She had to stay awake, to survive.

And she would.

For Lucas. For his baby. For the life that he deserved to have and for the life that she'd promised Marissa that she would give him.

She silently cursed the stupid things she'd said to Lucas so that he'd leave. *I'm a big girl. Trust me, I can take care of myself.*

But she obviously couldn't.

Not only had she allowed two kidnappers to break into her home, she hadn't even been armed at the time. Instead, she'd been fighting back tears over Lucas's visit. Crying instead of grabbing her gun. And that was despite every primitive alarm going off in her head that something wasn't right. So much for listening to her gut. She'd be lucky to get the baby and herself out of this alive.

She lifted her left eyelid a fraction and saw where they were taking her. In the direction of the lake. Probably to the road that circled it so they could escape. Or else they planned to drown her. But Kylie pushed that frightening thought aside. If they'd wanted her dead, they probably already would have killed her. And they certainly wouldn't have come prepared to chloroform her.

Of course, she couldn't rule out that they were taking her to a secondary crime scene, a place where they could finish her off and dispose of her body without leaving any forensic evidence behind.

She added some mental groans to her mental profanity. She couldn't give in to these what-ifs and worst-case scenarios. If she did, she'd likely die.

Instead, she focused on the lake, on what she knew about it. After all, it was as familiar to her as her own home. It was where she took daily walks and did most of her writing. She figured that the men had parked off the road. If she got a break, one little distraction, she could dive into the water, and, uh…

Probably drown.

Yes. Drown.

Another mental groan. She was already so dizzy that she couldn't stay focused. Heaven only knew what would happen to her in the water.

Okay. Plan A was discarded. She moved on to Plan B. Too bad she couldn't think of one. Sweet heaven, her head was spinning and she felt on the verge of throwing up. Still, she fought through that haze and forced herself to think. She had to come up with something.

The thudding noise and the howl of pain jarred open her eyes. Not that she could see much. But she was able to determine that the other man was no longer in front of them. He was on the ground, writhing and groaning.

"What the hell?" the one holding her growled, a split second before he let go of her.

Kylie managed to protect her stomach and break the fall with her hands. She immediately got to her knees so that she could get away and scurried behind a tree. It wasn't easy but, dragging her way through the underbrush and soggy dead leaves, she somehow got there. It took her a few seconds to realize that her captor wasn't coming after her.

It took a few more to realize why.

One of the men was still on the ground. And he was the one who was moaning and holding on to his leg. However, the other guy aimed his gun at a shadowy figure that appeared between two trees.

Lucas.

He'd come back.

"Lucas!" she called out to warn him. It wasn't her best effort. More breath than voice. She sounded drunk and, worse, felt that way, too.

Still, he reacted. Lucas darted to her side just as the guy fired at him. The shot blasted through the woods, clipping a tree and spraying splinters and bark. The sound was deafening and shook her to the core. Not just because it drilled home the danger for herself and the baby, but because Lucas was now in danger, as well.

Oh, God.

And she was responsible for him being here.

If he were hurt, or worse, it would be her fault. Kylie wasn't sure she could live with that. She'd already caused enough devastation in his life.

Frantically, she searched the ground, looking for anything she could use to defend them. The dizziness and nausea didn't help. Still, she kept searching, raking aside the leaves, and finally came up with a thick, long tree limb. It wouldn't be much protection against a semiautomatic, but if she got close enough, she could do some damage.

Well, maybe.

With her focus fading in and out, she probably wouldn't be much of a threat even if she'd had a loaded gun.

She peeked out from behind the tree. Neither of the kidnappers was anywhere in sight. Great. Just great. They could come at her and Lucas from any direction and, considering that she could only move slowly, she'd be a sitting duck.

"Shhh." The sound was barely audible, but it was the only warning she got before Kylie felt a rough hand clamp over her mouth.

She automatically struggled, trying to defend herself with the tree branch, but the man—and it was definitely a man—pulled her to him. Right against his solid, rock-hard body. Her face landed against a buckskin coat. A familiar coat.

With an equally familiar scent.

"It's me," Lucas whispered. Without making a

sound, he eased forward and positioned himself in front of her, using his body as a shield to protect her.

Kylie quietly laid down the branch and checked to make sure he wasn't injured. Even with the full hunter's moon, she couldn't see much. Well, not much except the stalwart, determined expression on Lucas's face.

Lucas didn't take his vigilant gaze off their surroundings. He reached over, the fingertips of his left hand skimming over her stomach.

The baby kicked.

Right on the spot where Lucas was touching her.

If Lucas had noticed it, he didn't say anything. Instead, he readjusted her robe. Putting it back in place. Most likely so that she'd stay warm. In all the chaos, she hadn't realized that the only thing between her stomach and the cold night air was a thin white cotton gown.

"Are you okay?" he whispered.

She hadn't been injured in the fall, but every muscle in her body was already aching and stiff from the fight and the adrenaline. Then, there was the chloroform or whatever had been on that cloth. It might be hours, or days, before she knew what effect that would have on her. And the baby. Especially the baby.

"I'm okay."

And she prayed that was true.

Her reassurance didn't do a thing to ease his vigilance. He kept his Glock aimed and ready. And she knew for a fact that he had a lethal aim. She only hoped that it was enough to get them out of this alive.

Kylie pulled in her breath and waited. She listened carefully, but all she could hear was the wind rattling through the towering oak trees. Reality quickly began to sink in. Yes, Lucas was there, and he was armed. And he was good. But sometimes *good* just wasn't good enough.

Frowning, scowling really, Lucas brushed his knuckles over her lips. Barely a touch. Kylie flinched at the contact. However, she welcomed it in a weird, surreal sort of way. Human contact, even if it happened to be from Lucas, felt pretty comforting.

"You're humming," he whispered. "Out loud."

Kylie stopped, considered that. "Am I?" she whispered back.

A crisp nod. "'Jingle Bells.'"

No surprise there. Humming perky, out-of-season tunes was her way of dealing with stress. And right now, she was dealing with a lot of stress.

"Sorry," she offered, and she clamped her teeth over her lip to make sure it didn't happen again.

But her stress level soared when she heard someone moving through the woods.

Her heart began to pound even harder than before. She forced herself to breathe normally so that she wouldn't hyperventilate.

Beside her, Lucas didn't react, didn't move a muscle. Definitely no threat of hyperventilation for him. Everything in him seemed to still, like a jungle cat waiting to move in for the kill.

The sounds continued. They were closer now. Definitely footsteps. Despite the roar in her ears, she could measure the pace of whoever was walking. Slow, methodical steps. Not from the side, but from behind them.

God, from behind them.

They were about to be ambushed.

Lucas whipped around and fired a shot. "I'm Sheriff Lucas Creed," he called out, his voice even more of a warning than the bullet he'd just fired. "I know your partner's injured because he's got my knife in his leg. My advice? Surrender. He needs medical attention now."

The footsteps stopped.

And the silence returned.

Long, agonizing moments.

She waited. Trying to stay conscious and to still her body as Lucas had done his. Of course, the baby chose that moment to kick like an NFL punter. Kylie slid her hand over her stomach and rubbed gently.

Lucas's gaze came to hers. He didn't speak, but his left eyebrow slid up. It was a question. *Are you truly okay?* That unsaid question touched her.

Until she made the connection.

His concern wasn't for her per se. This was some kind of transference because of his own impending fatherhood. Of course, he had no way of knowing that the kicking baby was his *baby*.

She'd done everything within her power to keep it a secret. And she would continue to do that. Not just through the pregnancy and delivery, but forever.

The thought of that broke her heart. She could never let this child know that she was his or her mother.

Never.

Sometimes, like now, that seemed too high a price to pay, but then she'd created a huge debt because of that fatal shooting three years ago. And she'd made that promise to Marissa. This was the one way she could repay Marissa and Lucas. Her heart would be broken, but his would finally be healed.

"They're gone," she heard Lucas say.

Kylie listened and heard the sound of a vehicle on the lake road. Driving away.

Or better yet—*getting away.*

"You have to go after them," she whispered frantically.

But just saying those few words robbed her of what little energy she had left.

"No," Lucas answered. "I can't leave you. Not without backup."

Part of her greatly appreciated that. Especially since she was unarmed, barely conscious and a couple of steps past being defenseless. But another part of her, the former cop part, knew that without suspects in custody, she might never learn why they'd come after. The two ski-mask-wearing men might simply disappear.

Which would create a real nightmare for her.

She'd always be wondering, worrying when, where and if they'd strike again. What little peace of mind she had would be a thing of the past.

With that realization, Kylie gave up the fight.

Because she had no choice, she leaned her head against the tree, and the murkiness and the winter night closed in around her.

Chapter Four

"This isn't necessary," Kylie grumbled. Again.

Lucas ignored her. Again.

Balancing the cell phone that he had sandwiched between his shoulder and his ear, he gently deposited Kylie onto the paper-covered examining table. She was still groggy, but not so groggy that it prevented her from insisting that she could have walked into the clinic on her own.

Yeah, right.

She was wearing only those flimsy socks. And the temperature had been below freezing. The ground had been hard and slick with frost. Still, if Lucas hadn't been concerned that she might fall flat on her face, he would have given in to her protests and let her test her theory concerning her walking capabilities. But a fall might have injured her baby. Or even her. Despite how he felt about Kylie, Lucas hadn't been about to risk that.

"You can wait out there, Lucas," Dr. Finn McGrath insisted. And to clarify what he meant by *out there,*

Finn hitched his thumb in the direction of the empty reception area just outside the examining room.

"She'll be okay, right?" Lucas asked.

That earned him a flat look from Finn, a man he'd known all his thirty-one years of life. His best friend.

"I know, I know. Your psychic skills are a little rusty," Lucas jested.

"But you're in luck," Finn replied. "I'm not too rusty in the medical department."

Lucas appreciated his friend's attempt to settle him down, but the attempt was wasted. "They drugged her with something," he explained.

"Yeah. Figured that out." Finn put a hand on Lucas's back to get him moving. "I'll examine her. But since examining her means making sure she doesn't have any injuries beneath her gown, I don't think Kylie will want you to be in the room for that. Doubt you'll want to be there, either."

No. He didn't. And it made Lucas more than a little uncomfortable to think of Kylie and what was beneath that gown. Best to think of her only as his former deputy.

As his enemy.

As his most recent 911 call.

Unfortunately, it was impossible to leave out the part about her being pregnant and apparently in a whole boatload of danger.

"I need to bag her clothes," Lucas reminded Finn. "I can send them to the crime lab in Austin to see if they recover any trace evidence."

"Yes, I figured that out, too." Finn pressed a little harder on Lucas's back. "Don't worry. Clothes will be bagged and tagged, and I'll scrounge up something around here for her to wear."

Lucas nodded and stepped into the reception area. He hadn't really noticed it on the way in—mainly because his brain had been too occupied with Kylie and her need for medical attention—but he saw the recent changes Finn had made in the office. A wall mural of a serene pasture dotted with bluebonnets and longhorns. A children's corner stocked with all sorts of toys and books. Gone was the old loveseat, and in its place were four navy leather chairs. Nice ones. But Lucas was too antsy to make use of the chairs. And he was too tired to pace. So, he leaned against the wall and waited.

He glanced at the tiny screen on his phone to determine if he was still on hold. He was connected, which meant Sheriff Knight was no doubt trying to come up with a situation report on the crime scene, so Lucas used the downtime to try to figure out what the heck was going on.

Two men, both armed, had tried to kidnap Kylie.

Why?

They hadn't wanted to kill her, that's for sure, or she would have been dead before he could have gotten to her. Not exactly something he cared to admit. But he knew it was true. After mentally reconstructing the possible scenarios, Lucas figured the kidnappers had had more than ample opportunity to murder Kylie while she was still inside her house. But instead, they'd taken her outside. Toward the lake. Probably to some waiting vehicle.

And that's where his scenario reconstruction dropped like a sack of rocks.

Once he'd carried Kylie to his truck so he could get her to the doctor's office, he'd called Dillon Knight, the sheriff from the neighboring town, and asked him to proceed with backup to Kylie's house. Knight's initial report was that there were no signs of the kidnappers or a ransom note. Plus, Lucas knew Kylie wasn't a good candidate for a ransom demand since she wasn't wealthy. That ruled out kidnapping for money.

It didn't rule out kidnapping for other reasons.

Revenge. Criminal intent. Perhaps even a way of silencing or punishing her. He'd need to narrow down the possible motives so he could narrow down the list of possible suspects.

"How far along are you in the pregnancy?" Finn asked Kylie.

Even though Lucas didn't hear Kylie's softly delivered answer, the question sent Lucas's blood pressure up a significant notch. He glanced into the examining room. Finn hadn't shut the door all the way—it was open just a few inches—but it gave Lucas a much clearer view than he wanted.

Kylie had her gaze fastened toward the ceiling, and her left arm was angled so that the back of her hand rested against her forehead. Finn had indeed pushed her gown up to her waist, exposing her bare legs. And her panties. Cotton. Nothing provocative.

Lucas mentally repeated that to himself.

And wondered why it didn't sink in.

Finn had a stethoscope pressed to Kylie's stomach, which was also bare, and after a couple of moments, he gave an approving nod.

Finn's gaze met Lucas's and with that brief look, Finn conveyed his concern. His empathy.

And his questions.

Finn knew the hell that Lucas and Kylie had gone through. And he also knew that Kylie had had a huge part in creating that particular hell. Now, Finn was probably wondering how Lucas was dealing with the fact that Kylie was pregnant.

Lucas wasn't dealing with it well.

"Is the baby okay?" Kylie asked.

Finally, she was speaking normally. No slurred words. No mumbling. Lucas felt relief. Then anger for feeling relief that she was apparently all right. Then guilt for feeling the anger.

Oh, man.

Much more of this, and he'd need therapy.

"The baby's got a steady, solid heartbeat," Finn relayed in a voice loud enough so that Lucas could hear. "Your heartbeat's solid as well, Kylie. No visible signs of injury other than a few bruises and scrapes."

So she wasn't seriously hurt. That was something at least.

"Lucas?" he heard the person on the other end of the phone line say. Sheriff Dillon Knight. Lucas welcomed the intrusion. Heck, at this point he'd welcome anything as long as he didn't have to think about Kylie, her baby and what was going on in that examining room.

"You found something?" Lucas asked, tuning out what Kylie was now saying to Finn.

"Nothing good. It looks as if the men made a get-away on the old lake road."

That's what Lucas had figured, too. "There will be tire tracks. And blood. I used my knife on one of them, and he probably left a trail of his DNA all the way to the lake."

"I saw that. We've got the area cordoned off so the county forensic guys can come out and have a look. Maybe they'll find a print or two. Or else they can run the blood and find a match in CODIS."

CODIS, the Combined DNA Index System. A data bank of sorts. But the only way there'd be a match would be if the wounded would-be kidnapper's DNA was already on file in the system.

Which wasn't too much of a long shot.

After all, neither man had been tentative about committing a felony. They'd probably done something criminal before. Or at least, Lucas hoped they had. Because a match in CODIS would give him a name. And with a name, he might be able to figure out why this had happened. That was vital; he needed to solve this case so there'd be no reason for him to be around Kylie.

"I'll keep you posted," Sheriff Knight told him as he ended the call.

Lucas slipped his phone into his jacket pocket, turned back to the doorway and saw Finn standing there, his hands bracketed on each side of the jamb. In physical appearance, they were practically opposites. Finn, with his moon-blond hair, blue eyes and his natural surfer-dude tan. Definitely not a typical Texas cowboy. Lucas knew the man didn't even own a pair of boots. No Stetson, either. And Finn liked to boast that he'd never been within ten feet of a horse. Even when he wore green scrubs, like now, he still managed to look as if he'd just stepped off a surfboard.

"She'll be okay," Finn let him know. He handed Lucas a clear plastic bag that contained Kylie's clothes. "I drew some blood so I can figure out what they used to sedate her. But she should have a checkup by her regular OB. She should have an ultrasound, too."

Lucas glanced over Finn's shoulder and saw Kylie. She was now wearing a set of Finn's scrubs. And yet another pair of socks.

"You can't do the ultrasound here?" Lucas asked.

"Sorry. Don't have the equipment." Finn hooked the stethoscope around his neck, yawned and rubbed his eyes. "There are a lot of advantages to living in a small town like Fall Creek, but we're Podunkville as far as that type of medical service. She'll have to go to a larger facility for it."

Lucas considered it and mentally cursed. "It was

Kylie's trip into San Antonio that might have led to the kidnapping attempt. Kylie had said something about two men possibly following her home."

"Yes," Kylie verified. "They did."

"That means a trip back into the city isn't a good idea," Lucas concluded.

At least, not alone. However, it wasn't a trip Lucas intended to make with her. He'd have to turn this over to a deputy or else Sheriff Knight. This eerie proximity with Kylie Monroe was a lot more than he could handle.

"I'll drive her in the morning," Finn volunteered, probably sensing what was on Lucas's mind. "I have a colleague who manages one of those back-to-nature kind of birthing facilities just outside San Antonio. It's in the country. Very serene. Off the beaten path. And private. He'll let me use his ultrasound machine. We'll keep everything hush-hush."

Lucas nodded, conveying his thanks. Hopefully, a private facility also meant a safe one.

When there was the sound of movement in the examining room, Finn turned, angling his body so that Lucas and he had a clear view of Kylie. She tried to get up...and failed. With a groan, she eased back down onto the table.

"They used chloroform on me, didn't they?" Kylie asked. She didn't wait for an answer. "Will it hurt the baby?"

"Probably not," Finn answered. "We'll know more in a day or two when I get back the test results."

Another soft groan. But a groan wasn't her only reaction. A tear slid down her cheek, and she quickly swiped it away. "Did anyone catch the men who did this to me?"

Finn stepped aside. That was Lucas's cue to fill her in and ask a few questions so he'd have info for the report he would have to make. "They're still at large."

"Oh, that's wonderful," she mumbled.

Lucas ignored the sarcasm and got to work. "Did you get a good look at either of the men?"

Judging from the way her forehead bunched up, she considered that. "No. They were both wearing ski masks. Both dressed in all black. One was about six-one, the other about two inches taller. The taller one had light gray eyes. And he said something like, 'Don't hurt the kid or her. We're to deliver her to the boss. So they can talk.'"

"Talk?" Lucas repeated skeptically.

"I didn't believe that's what they had on their minds, either." She tried to sit up again. This time, she succeeded. Well, for the most part. Kylie wobbled, and she grasped the sides of the examining table. Her gaze came to his. "I'm sorry, Lucas. I'm so sorry."

He didn't want her apology. Nor did he want her to specify *why* she was sorry. Maybe it was for Marissa. Or maybe it was because she believed she'd placed him in danger with her 911 call. It was true that she had, but being placed in danger came with his job.

"I've got to phone a few people and take care of the

arrangements for the ultrasound," Finn said, making his way out of the room.

Leaving Lucas alone with Kylie.

Lucas decided the best approach to this was the most obvious one—to continue his interview. He was the sheriff, after all, and he'd questioned many victims of many crimes. He would treat this one no differently than the others.

He stopped and admitted that it was a sad day in a man's life when he started lying to himself.

He had no choice but to treat this case differently. Because this case involved Kylie.

She shook her head. Winced. Wobbled again. Flashed him when she tried to use her leg to maintain her balance. She probably would have fallen if Lucas hadn't reached out and snagged her shoulders.

"Thanks." She dropped her head against his right arm. Eased against him.

As if she belonged there.

And for some stupid reason, he didn't move. He let her stay.

She was shaking, and she looked up at him. Her eyes were ripe with fatigue, spent adrenaline and the after-effects of the kidnappers' drug.

"I'm scared," she whispered. It was an admission he'd never heard Kylie make. And it was true. He could see that stark fear on her face. He could feel it in her. "They could have killed us. You, me, the baby. All three of us."

"But they didn't."

There was no indication in her body language that she believed him. "And here I was so full of myself. So cocky about how I didn't anyone want to protect me. God, Lucas." Her voice broke and became a hoarse sob. More tears came. "I was wrong, and that mistake could have cost you everything again. They could have killed your baby."

His heart actually skipped a beat.

Your baby.

Lucas opened his mouth to correct her. And might have done that if he hadn't felt Kylie freeze. She went completely stiff; that extreme reaction had him staring down at her.

She pulled back, meeting his gaze head-on. In the depths of all that blue, Lucas saw something in her eyes that he didn't understand.

He shook his head.

"It's true," Kylie said, as if that explained everything.

It took him a moment just to ask what he needed to ask. "What's true?"

"The only reason I'm telling you this is because I'm afraid I can't protect this baby by myself. Not now. Not with those men still out there."

"What are you telling me exactly?" Lucas tried to brace himself for the answer. Judging from her expression, he couldn't possibly brace himself enough.

A moment later, Kylie confirmed that.

"When you applied for a surrogate, I pulled some strings. Called in a few favors." He watched the words form on her lips, and each one stabbed through him. "Lucas, I'm your surrogate, and this baby I'm carrying is yours."

WELL, THAT IMPROMPTU confession cleared Kylie's head.

The residual effects of the kidnappers' drug vanished, leaving her with vision and a brain that was a little too clear. That clarity allowed her to see the thunderstruck expression on Lucas's face.

"My baby?" he mumbled.

She watched that register. First, he shook his head. Stared at her. Shook his head again.

Then it sank in.

He stepped back, his chest pumping as if he were suddenly starved for air. He tried to speak. Couldn't. He looked as if he were on the verge of seriously losing it. Kylie reached for him, but he put up his hands, palms out, in a back-off gesture.

"Why?" he finally asked.

She didn't know how he had managed to speak. His teeth were practically clamped together, and his jaw muscles had seemingly turned to iron. But those responses were tame compared to that look in his eyes. There was fire mixed with all those shades of brown. Fire and brimstone.

"Why?" Kylie repeated. "I've asked myself that more than a few times."

"Is this some kind of warped punishment?" Lucas's anger chilled his voice. "Your way of torturing me?"

She'd anticipated a few of the things Lucas might say if he ever learned the truth, but that hadn't been one of them. "No. God, no. It's because of what happened to Marissa."

"Don't. I don't want to talk about her."

Kylie didn't even consider heeding his warning. Despite his glare. Despite his defensive posture. They had to get a few things straight. "I did this because of what Marissa said when she was dying. 'Don't let my death kill Lucas. Look after him. Help him heal. Make sure he's happy.' And that's what I promised her I would do. I owed her that promise. But you wouldn't let me help you."

"I didn't *want* you to do any of those things for me," Lucas protested, stabbing his accusing index finger in her direction. "I didn't want your help. I still don't. In fact, the only thing I wanted from you was never to see you again."

Now, that she'd expected him to say. Too bad she hadn't planned a perfectly worded response. Too bad that his words hurt.

"You think this was an easy decision for me to make?" she asked. "Well, it wasn't. I agonized over it. I'm twenty-nine years old, Lucas, and haven't had a relationship with a man in years. This may be the only baby I ever have, and it's not even mine. Hear that? It's not a baby I can hope that you'll share with me."

Nothing she said soothed him. In fact, it had the opposite effect. His jaw muscles jerked. And it seemed as if Lucas were about to let go of the choke hold he had on his anger and other emotions.

"And at no point during this monumental decision-making process did it occur to you to ask me if I wanted *you* for a surrogate?" he stormed. "No. That would have too reasonable. Something a sane, normal person would have done. And you know what I would have said if you'd asked, Kylie? I would have told you that there's no way in hell I want you to be the mother of my child."

Oh, that stung.

Mercy.

And here she thought she was somewhat immune to anything Lucas could say to her. She was obviously wrong.

"I made a promise to Marissa," Kylie reminded him. Because that was the true bottom line of why she'd made her decision. Yes, her guilt had contributed to it. So had her need to somehow pay for her mistake. But if Marissa hadn't asked, Kylie wouldn't have become Lucas's surrogate. "And I always keep my promises."

"Oh, that's a good one." He took several steps toward her and got right in her face. "What about the promise to keep the citizens of Fall Creek safe? What about your sworn oath to follow regs? Regs you ignored when you went after those two men who robbed the convenience store? Was it worth it, Kylie? Was Marissa's and my baby's lives worth catching two scumbags who'd stolen a hundred and twenty-three dollars?"

Kylie had no answer for that, and she'd tried for nearly three years to find one. She'd made a fatal mistake that day. Not waiting for backup. Proceeding on foot after two armed suspects. Though waiting for backup might not have changed the outcome, it was a mistake she'd tried to live with.

So far, she hadn't been successful.

She wasn't holding out hope that she would succeed any time soon. Because of Marissa's death, she turned in her badge. Resigned. She'd quit a job she loved. But Kylie was under no illusions that her resignation would atone for what she'd done.

"Look, I know this isn't my business," she heard Finn say. He had come back into the room, stepping between Lucas and her. "But you're both my friends, and I won't stand here and let you two rip each other apart. Besides, I'd like to get some sleep. My advice is that both of you should quit talking and instead start trying to figure out what you're going to do. Not about the baby," he quickly added. "Leave that for a day when tempers have settled a bit. I'm concerned about a more immediate problem here."

Kylie waited until Lucas turned his attention from her and aimed it at Finn before she followed suit. She also tried to let what Finn had said sink in. Yes. They did have a more immediate problem than her secret surrogacy.

Finn's hands went to his hips. "Let me insult your intelligence and summarize the situation, Lucas. Someone tried to kidnap Kylie tonight. She's possibly still in danger. And that baby she's carrying is yours. My advice—bury the hatchet. Not in her back, either. Bury it and get on with what you know you have to do."

Kylie figured it was a good time for her to sit there and shut up. Lucas must have decided the same thing because the conversation ground to a halt. Seconds ticked by, practically turning into minutes, before Finn cursed.

"All right. Be that way. Since it obviously isn't safe or prudent for Kylie to go home, and since I doubt she wants to sleep in the jail or on that examining table, you should take her to your ranch, Lucas."

"No!" Kylie and Lucas said in unison.

Finn shrugged and directed his attention to Lucas. "Well, I can't bring Kylie with me to my house. I can't defend her against kidnappers and other assorted felons. I don't even own a gun. And besides, protecting her is your job."

When Lucas didn't respond other than with a lethal glare, Finn huffed. "Since you're a good sheriff, and since I know you're not an ass, I'm trying hard to figure out why you're hesitating. Is it public opinion? Gossip, maybe?" He stopped, as if considering that. "Please don't tell me you're concerned how your former sister-in-law would feel about Kylie staying at the ranch."

Now, it was Lucas's turn to huff. "Cordelia doesn't make decisions for me."

"That's never stopped her from trying," Finn mumbled. He grabbed Lucas's hand and plopped it against Kylie's stomach. "But whatever's causing you to hesitate, forget it. Do what you've sworn to do. Protect her. Protect your baby."

Lucas's hand was stiff. Even through the cotton scrubs, she could feel the calluses he'd earned the hard way—by working on his ranch. His touch stayed rigid, defensive. He closed his eyes for a moment. Swallowed hard.

Then, something happened.

His touch suddenly wasn't so hard. Wasn't so defensive.

Finn backed away. Lucas's hand stayed put. And his fingers moved gently over her stomach. Not far. Mere fractions of an inch. He didn't make a sound. Didn't say word.

But their gazes met.

And in that gaze, Kylie saw what was going on. Pain, yes. That was a given. But there was more. That gentleness wasn't about the pain, but rather about the life growing inside her.

"My baby," he said under his breath. "Why?" Not an accusation this time, but a plea.

She waited a moment, to clear that sudden lump in her throat. While she was at it, she prayed she wouldn't disgrace herself again by crying. "I wanted to try to give you back what I took from you."

He waited a moment, as well. Staring at her. Really

staring. He pulled his hand away, and she immediately felt the loss of his body heat. Something stirred deep down within her. An ache. A longing. A…need.

Oh, great.

Kylie quickly shoved that ache, that longing, that blasted need aside. And silently cursed that feeling. She couldn't associate any of those things with Lucas. Heck, it was best not to associate anything at all with him.

But shoving it aside didn't make it so.

She felt that punch. It had to be lust. Temporary, fleeting lust brought out by hormones and adrenaline. It just had to be that, and that alone.

Because there was no other alternative.

"So, I'll send the bagged clothes to the crime lab for you," Finn interrupted. He grabbed a leather coat from the rack in the reception area and draped it over her shoulders. "And you'll take Kylie to your ranch?"

But it wasn't exactly a question. More like an impatient reminder that he couldn't go home until they'd cleared out of his clinic.

Lucas tore his gaze from hers. "She'll come with me," he confirmed to Finn.

And he didn't leave room for argument.

Not that she could argue, anyway. After all, her number one priority had to be the baby. To keep the baby safe. And to do that, *she* had to stay safe.

However, Kylie wasn't sure what she feared more— the kidnappers returning or spending what was left of the night under the same roof with Lucas. The first was downright dangerous. And the second—staying with Lucas—well, after what she'd just experienced, it was a danger of a different kind. Still, it was a risk she had to take.

She didn't protest when Lucas scooped her up in his arms and carried her outside to his truck.

Chapter Five

Lucas kept his attention fixed on the two-lane road that led from town to his ranch. It was nearly three in the morning, and there was no traffic. Not even an occasional deer or coyote to give them a diversion.

Just Kylie and him.

And within five minutes, she would be inside his house and well on her way to sleeping in one of his beds.

Nothing about that particular scenario pleased him.

Well, nothing except the part about keeping her safe. Finn was right. That was his job as sheriff, and he couldn't pick and choose his cases.

Even if that's exactly what he wanted to do.

"I would say thanks for doing this, but it'd probably just irritate you," Kylie commented.

She was right.

Lucas hoped his silence conveyed that.

"Okay, so a thank-you is off-limits," she continued a moment later. "Ditto for Marissa. I guess we could talk about the baby—"

"The baby's off-limits, too."

For now, anyway. However, it couldn't stay that way for long. Someway, somehow, he'd have to come to terms with the bombshell that Kylie had delivered back at the clinic.

Lucas, I'm your surrogate, and this baby I'm carrying is yours.

He shook his head. Coming to terms with that would take a miracle.

For nearly three years, his thoughts of Kylie had been churning with anger and bitterness, and that was putting it mildly. Now what was he supposed to do? Put all that hurt and fury behind him and just accept what she'd done?

What she had done was deceive him.

She'd gone behind his back. *Pulled some strings,* she'd said. And she had done all of that so she could get pregnant with his child.

Oh, man.

Part of him was down-on-his-knees humbled by that. Another part was even thankful. Because he wanted this child more than anything. But what he couldn't deal with was this baby would always have a link with Kylie. Her DNA. Her biological child just as much as his.

Hell.

How was he supposed to get past that?

Kylie. The mother of his child. A person he didn't want to be linked with—for anything.

Other than their brief history of working together, they didn't have anything in common. She was a neo-hippy, for heaven sakes. Raised by a love-bead-wearing grandmother, Meg, whose claim to fame was that she'd once made out with Bob Dylan in some coffeehouse in New York City. That was probably wishful thinking on her part. Meg had been into fantasy. Unlike Kylie. Yes, Kylie ate tofu and sprouts and had a Save The Wolves bumper sticker on her environmentally friendly car. But she was real. The kind of woman you could count on to tell you the truth.

Even when the truth hurt like hell.

That's why this lie stung so much. The one thing he'd always been sure of when it came to Kylie was that he'd get the truth. Yet, here for four and a half months, she'd lied by omission.

"Then can we talk about those kidnappers?" Kylie asked.

Lucas didn't veto that one. In fact, it was the only common ground he wanted with Kylie right now because it pertained to the case.

"Since the two men planned to take me to their boss *to talk,*" she said, "it's my guess that this has something to do with the article I wrote about illegal surrogacy."

That was his guess, too, especially since there'd been no ransom note. "What made you decide to write that article anyway?"

"Kismet." She sighed. "Or maybe it was rotten luck.

Right after I'd been inseminated...sorry. That wasn't an intentional reference to the baby."

Maybe not intentional, but it was a reference. Lucas couldn't disregard the fact that Kylie had been inseminated. With his semen. A totally impersonal act. As was the entire surrogacy procedure. Yet, it'd resulted in something that seemed to be the ultimate in intimacy.

A pregnancy.

"Anyway, I met this pregnant woman at the clinic," Kylie continued. "A girl, really. Her name is Tiffany Smith. She was in the ladies' room, and we struck up a conversation. She was barely seventeen, Lucas. Definitely underage. She admitted that she was a homeless runaway."

"And this Tiffany was there at the clinic because she was a surrogate?"

She nodded. "She was maybe five or six months pregnant and there to pick up her monthly stipend. She said that a man who worked for a lawyer first approached her about surrogacy when she still living on the street. He offered her money and a place to live if she'd have a baby for a couple who desperately wanted a child. I called an old P.I. friend, told him about Tiffany, and he did some checking for me. He couldn't find her. Coincidence? I doubt it. I think the person who hired her didn't want anyone to find out she was underage so they hid her."

Kylie turned in the seat, angling her body to face him. It wasn't an especially unusual move.

Except the moonlight seemed to turn into a friggin' spotlight.

He could clearly see her midsection, and because the bulky black leather coat had gaped open, he could see the outline of her stomach. Specifically, the bulge created by the pregnancy. There was a baby inside that bulge. *His baby.*

Lucas forced his attention back to the road and their conversation.

"You think the lawyer Tiffany Smith spoke about is Isaac Dupont?" he asked.

She made a sound of agreement. "Tiffany said the man, the go-between, dropped by a lawyer's office over in Alamo Heights. He had her wait in the car, so she never saw the lawyer in question. Plus, she didn't know the specific street but was able to give a description. I drove over there, and Dupont's office is right there, just as she described it."

It was a start for circumstantial evidence. "But you don't have concrete proof that he was behind this illegal surrogacy?"

"I don't have any positive proof, but I discovered that Dupont handled the adoption of one other medically unfit surrogate. When I called to ask him about it, he threatened me with a lawsuit and hung up on me. That in itself doesn't mean he's guilty, and that's why I only alluded to Dupont and the clinic director in my article. I mentioned that a prominent Alamo Heights attorney had handled some questionable adoptions linked to equally questionable surrogates at a downtown clinic. *Alluded,*" she repeated. "Don't you just love that word? It's supposed to be clinical, as in a journalist can *allude* without putting the publication or herself at risk. Ha. It doesn't feel very clinical or safe now."

No. It didn't. But then to Isaac Dupont, an insinuation was probably the same as an outright accusation. Leave it to Kylie to go after one of the most ruthless attorneys and businessmen in the state. Dupont had a take-no-prisoners reputation, and even though the man had been implicated in other activities, such as suspicious adoptions, none of the rumors or speculation had ever led to a real investigation.

Until now.

Lucas figured SAPD would want to question Kylie and check out the crime scene—especially after the kidnapping attempt. Of course, it would be a real coup if SAPD could also link those two would-be kidnappers to Dupont. Unfortunately, if Dupont was behind this, all those potential questions and attempts to link him to the attempted kidnapping would put Kylie in even more danger.

First thing in the morning, he'd make some calls and see if he could arrange protective custody for her. That would solve both of their problems. Because Lucas figured she didn't want to stay with him any more than he wanted to be with her.

He made the last turn to his ranch, crossed the cattle guard and brought the truck to a stop in front of his house. He waited a moment, checking to make sure everything looked normal. It did. The only thing abnormal was the whirlwind of emotions he was experiencing.

Dreading the next few hours, Lucas exited the truck, but Kylie got out before he could make it to the passenger's side. She even took a few steps, her socks lightly crunching on the frosted ground. Not only that, she wobbled, reaching out to grab something. But all she caught was air. He picked her up so that she wouldn't fall.

"This *really* isn't necessary," she complained.

He ignored her and didn't waste any time walking through the yard and stepping onto the porch. Kylie immediately slid out of his grip. But not before he felt the soft thump. It had come from her stomach and landed against his chest.

"It's the baby," she explained. She seemed embarrassed. Or something. She quickly pulled her coat closed.

Lucas unlocked the door, and they went inside. "The baby kicks a lot?" he asked.

She nodded.

Intrigued by that little flutter of movement, Lucas looked at her. It was only after he'd done it that he realized looking at her was a truly stupid idea.

Kylie looked up at him at the same moment that he looked down at her.

The air between them changed.

Not because either of them willed it. It just happened.

Their scents sort of intermingled. And he went from being intrigued by a baby's kick to being intrigued by the baby's mother. That wasn't even the worst part. The worst part was that Lucas was almost positive that Kylie was feeling the same thing.

He felt that little flicker of heat. A really bad kind of heat. The kind that could only happen with physical attraction. And he prayed that little flicker didn't turn into a full-blown flame.

"Well, crud," she mumbled. Then, she groaned. "Would it help if I told you what's going on here is a primal instinct that neither of us have any control over? Because this is your child, you feel this innate familiarity or something. And I feel this sicko kind of need to have you protect me. Probably something to do with continuation of the human race."

"Well, that certainly takes the emotion out of it," Lucas lied.

Kylie shrugged. "I didn't figure we were ready to deal with the emotion. Besides, it's just pregnancy hormones."

"Pregnancy hormones," he repeated. "They must be a lot like male hormones—brainless."

And he quickly got his *brain* on something else.

"The guest room's down there." Lucas pointed to the last room at the end of the hall. "There should be a robe hanging in the closet if you need it. Oh, and if you're hungry, you know where the fridge is."

She ran her fingers over the silver-framed photo of

Marissa that was on the table next to the front door. "I know where just about everything is in this house," Kylie reminded him.

Yeah. She probably did. When Marissa was alive, Kylie was over at least a couple of times a month. Still, it seemed so off-kilter having her here.

Everything seemed off-kilter.

Especially him.

He suddenly wished he had livestock to tend, horses to feed. Anything that would give him a break from himself. But so that he'd have more time for the baby, he'd sold the livestock and all but one of his horses, which was literally out to pasture. One horse would hardly offer enough work to burn Kylie's scent from his brain.

"Lucas?" she said. "I just want you to know that this baby really is yours. I have no plans to keep it or the money that you paid for the surrogacy. I won't even be a part of your or your baby's life. Once I deliver, I'll give the child to you and then leave."

And with that, she turned and headed for the guest room.

It was a powerful declaration. One that soothed him far more than it should have. Still, Lucas latched onto it and tried to picture his future. He remembered why he'd wanted to become a father in the first place. Because he loved children. And he because he wanted a son or daughter of his own. He couldn't lose another child, and if that meant protecting a woman he loathed....

But he stopped there.

That *loathed* part was starting to fade. And it couldn't. It just couldn't.

He wasn't ready for it to fade.

Too much was coming at him too fast. The kidnapping attempt. Learning the truth about Kylie's pregnancy. The intense longing caused by such a simple thing as feeling the baby kick. His brainless reaction to Kylie.

Especially that last one.

Because his reaction to Kylie hadn't had anything to do with protecting her. Hormones, indeed. What he was feeling was hot and primal, and it was already simmering to the point where it felt as if it might boil over.

Disgusted with himself and his own body, he followed Kylie down the hall so he could get a few things straight. Unfortunately, she'd already shut the door to the guest room; unfortunately, he threw open that door without thinking. She'd taken off the coat that she'd borrowed from Finn and was about to pull back the covers. In those few brief seconds, before she could put her stoic mask back on, he saw the fatigue. The worry.

The vulnerability.

It was a challenge, but Lucas didn't let that vulnerability get in the way of what he had to say. Because this had to be said. "It doesn't matter that you're carrying my baby. Nothing is ever going to happen between us," he informed her. "Got that?"

She gave a crisp nod. "Got it." She paused for a heartbeat, then snagged his gaze. "But are you trying to convince me? Or are you trying to convince yourself?"

Chapter Six

Kylie winced as she dried off from her shower. Spent adrenaline could do all sorts of nasty things to the body. Sore muscles. Aches. Fatigue. A general sense of feeling yucky. She'd been lucky in her pregnancy not to experience the "pleasures" of morning sickness, but she thought her luck might run out this morning.

She reluctantly put the scrubs and socks back on and topped the outfit with the thick terry cloth robe she'd borrowed from the closet. Obviously, it was Lucas's robe but not one that he'd worn, because it still smelled new. Then, she didn't imagine that Lucas was the bathrobe type. Or the pajama type, for that matter.

Which got her thinking things better left unthought.

"Get your mind out of the gutter, Kylie," she mumbled.

She glanced at herself in the dresser mirror and didn't care for what she saw. The scrubs and the robe weren't exactly her first choice of attire. Ditto for the lack of makeup or grooming supplies. Still, the clothes and bare face would have to do until she could get back to her place and change before going into the birthing center for the ultrasound. There were probably some of Marissa's things still in the house—she doubted that Lucas would have gotten rid of all of them—but Kylie would have gone naked rather than wear Marissa's clothes. She'd already rubbed enough proverbial salt in Lucas's wounds without adding more.

It'd been a mistake to tell him that she was his surrogate. Kylie knew that *now*. Hindsight was such an annoyingly accurate thing. She should have just stuck with the plan: give birth, let the surrogacy agency deliver the baby to Lucas and then leave.

For good.

If she'd done that, Lucas might have been able to forget all about her. He might have eventually been able to forgive her, as well. But by telling him, she'd ruined everything. Would he ever be able to look at his baby's face and not remember that she was that child's mother?

Of course, there was a flip side to this particular question. If she hadn't told Lucas, who would have helped protect her? SAPD, maybe. But no one other than Lucas would have had a vested interest in keeping the baby safe. She wasn't invincible. And pride was something she couldn't afford to indulge in.

At least, that's the rationalization that kept going through her head.

However, Kylie had to ask herself if protecting the baby was the only reason she'd told Lucas. Or was there something else? Some subconscious motivation? She wanted to believe that her motives were pure. But the doubts were right there next to the rationalization and the unwholesome thoughts she was having about him.

Are you trying to convince me? Or are you trying to convince yourself?

Those were the smart-mouthed questions she'd tossed at Lucas just hours earlier when he'd stormed into the guest room. Now she had to wonder if she'd aimed those questions at the wrong person.

Since Kylie didn't really want to know the answer to that, she decided to concentrate on a way to put a speedy end to all to this. Once Finn had done the ultrasound, she would call her cousin in Houston. He was a P.I., and he would almost certainly let her stay with him until the police could catch the guys who had tried to kidnap her. Heck, maybe she'd even stay there until she had the baby. That way, it would insure that she and Lucas wouldn't have any more contact with each other.

She opened the bathroom door and heard Lucas moving around in the kitchen. He seemed to be talking on the phone. And cooking. She immediately got a whiff of coffee and, heaven forbid, bacon. Her stomach lurched, but Kylie ignored it and tried to hold her breath while she went into the kitchen to remind him that she needed to pick up some clothes from her house.

However, something that Lucas said stopped her in her tracks.

"That sounds like the same two men who tried to

kidnap Kylie. You said you saw them near the medical clinic?"

That was a temporary cure for her morning sickness. Instead of a lurch, Kylie's stomach tightened. If Lucas had sounded more urgent, then she would have started to hope and pray that the men were on the verge of being apprehended. But since Lucas was carefully forking out sizzling bacon from the black cast-iron skillet, it probably meant the caller was informing Lucas of a sighting after the fact.

A cold sighting.

Which was a misnomer. Because it was anything but cold for her.

"That was about an hour or so after Kylie and I left," Lucas said in response to the caller. "Did you see which direction they were headed in?" He paused. "If you remember anything else, give me a call."

Lucas slipped the phone back into its cradle, mounted on the wall, and glanced at her. "You heard?"

She nodded. "Who saw them?"

"The night security guard at the bank."

In other words, probably a reliable source. It told her two things—first, that the one man hadn't been so badly hurt that they'd had to flee the area to seek medical attention, and second, that the men weren't going to give up.

That knot in her stomach tightened.

"I don't have any tofu, yogurt or any of the other healthy stuff you like to eat, but there's coffee," Lucas advised her.

"No, thanks. I gave it up."

He blinked. "You quit drinking coffee?" Asked in the same tone as, Y*ou quit breathing?*

"The caffeine isn't good for the baby."

"Oh."

It was as if she'd stomped right on a raw nerve again. Of course, any conversation about the baby would likely be painful. She figured it would take Lucas time to accept this, but Kylie had to believe he would. After all, he did want to become a father, and she was offering the baby to him with no strings attached.

She was about to remind him that she needed to drop by her house, but the knock at the kitchen door stopped her. Not just a knock, either. One brief tap, and the door flew open.

"Brr. It's freezing. The front door was locked so I decided to come around to the back."

Kylie immediately recognized the voice. And the owner of the voice.

Cordelia Landrum.

Owner of the town's only women's clothing boutique. Marissa's sister. Lucas's former sister-in-law. And a general pain in the butt whom Kylie didn't want to face. Not this morning. Not any morning.

Cordelia was still brr-ing and briskly rubbing her kid gloved hands together when she entered. Her mouth was wide with a rose-slick smile—until her attention landed on Kylie, that is.

"What are you doing here?" Cordelia demanded.

Kylie had gotten warmer greetings from perps as she was arresting them. But that was to be expected. Cordelia and Kylie had never been friends, but Marissa's death had certainly made them enemies. It was a shame, because Cordelia looked so much like her sister. From her sleek strawberry-blond ponytail to those aristocratic mist-green eyes. If Cordelia weren't, well, Cordelia, then it might have been nice to have her around just because it would be like hanging on to a little piece of Marissa.

"Someone tried to kidnap Kylie last night," Lucas explained. "She's in my temporary protective custody."

And he hastily jumped right in there with that explanation, too. Probably because he didn't want Cordelia to think anything funny was going on.

Funny as in sexual.

Which wouldn't have been a totally absurd conclusion for Cordelia to draw since Kylie was wearing Lucas's robe while standing in the middle of his kitchen. Of course, because of Lucas's and her history, probably even Cordelia wouldn't believe that Lucas and she were lovers.

His explanation prompted Cordelia to give Kylie a once-over. That cool gaze slid from Kylie's still wet hair, past her stomach, all the way to her feet.

Wait a minute.

Kylie didn't miss the fact that Cordelia's gaze hadn't even paused, much less lingered, on her pregnant stomach. It was such an odd thing to bypass that Kylie glanced down to make sure she appeared as large as she felt.

Yep. Her pregnant belly was there. Totally visible. Not hidden one iota by the scrubs or the robe that she'd left untied.

"How long will she be here?" Cordelia asked Lucas.

Lucas calmly put the skillet into the sink. "I'm not sure."

That answer surprised Kylie almost as much as Cordelia's lack of response to the pregnancy. What the heck was going on? Had that chloroform and adrenaline fried a few of her brain cells?

"I don't want her here," Cordelia concluded. "This is my sister's house."

An easy comeback would have been for Kylie to remind her that it was Lucas's house, as well. But Kylie held her tongue. In the grand scheme of things, Cordelia's annoyance just wasn't very important. Not when someone wanted to kidnap her and do God knows what to her and the baby.

Cordelia took a step toward her. Because it seemed like a challenge and because she couldn't resist that, Kylie took a step toward her, as well.

They faced each other eye to eye.

"I'll call Lucas this afternoon," Cordelia informed her. "I'll expect you to be gone by then. If not, I'll do something about it. Understand?"

Kylie shook her head. "Not really. But that sounds like some kind of threat. Is it?"

"Cordelia," Lucas warned.

But if Cordelia had heard his warning, she showed

no signs of heeding it. She kept her focus on Kylie. "If you don't think I can make trouble for you, then think again."

Kylie considered just staying quiet, but her mouth didn't cooperate. "Cordelia, it really isn't necessary for you to keep reminding me just how much you hate me. You couldn't possibly hate me more than I hate myself."

"Don't bet on it." And with that chilly comeback, Cordelia turned, issued an equally chilly goodbye to Lucas from over her shoulder, and slammed the kitchen door behind her.

If Kylie hadn't been sure of what to do, she was after that exit. She had to get out of there.

Because Cordelia would cause problems for Lucas. And Lucas already had enough problems as it was. After all, the idea was to make him happy again. To heal his heart. To do what she'd promised Marissa that she would do. She couldn't very well heal anything if she was making him miserable.

"I'll call Finn to come and pick me up." Kylie walked toward the phone.

"You can't. He phoned while you were in the shower. One of the Krepner kids broke his arm in two places when he fell off his bunk bed. Finn said he needs to take care of that, and then he'll just meet us at the Brighton Medical Center around noon. He gave me directions."

Slowly, she turned back around to face him. "And you'll be taking me there," Kylie concluded. But before the last word left her mouth, she was already considering other options. *Any* other options.

"Don't even think about arguing. Those two men were near Finn's clinic. I don't think that's a coincidence, Kylie. They're looking for you. And they'll keep looking until they're caught."

She couldn't argue with that. It was the stuff nightmares were made of. Still, what she couldn't quite grasp was that Lucas didn't seem riled about spending what would no doubt be an entire morning with her.

"This new attitude of yours is because of the baby," Kylie said, more to herself than to him.

"Of course it is. What else would it be about?"

Nothing that she wanted to voice.

"I need to blow-dry my hair," she told him. "Give me fifteen minutes, and I'll be ready to leave."

Kylie walked out, intending to hurry back to the bathroom. Mainly because that whole bacon smell and the confrontation with Cordelia had sent her stomach into another tailspin. However, she stopped when she glanced out the sidelight windows that framed the front door.

The entire front yard and the driveway were covered with frost. It glistened in the morning light, making the ranch look like postcard material. What marred the pretty picture was Cordelia, who was still parked out front. Sitting in the driver's seat of her pricey red sports car. She had her head down, and she seemed to be talking to herself. Whatever she was saying obviously didn't please her because her expression was one of anger and....what? Frustration, maybe? Kylie couldn't quite make sense of it until Cordelia turned in her direction. And glared at her.

The emotion was anger. Pure, uncut anger.

A chill went through Kylie, and she didn't think it had to do with the temperature outside. That look on Cordelia's face said it all. Cordelia hated her. And that got Kylie thinking.

Had Cordelia already done something about that hatred?

After all, she hadn't even reacted to Kylie's pregnancy. Why? Why wouldn't she have shown at least some mild interest?

Because perhaps she already knew?

She considered that a moment, and then she took her musings one step further. If Cordelia had somehow learned about the baby, then what? She wouldn't be pleased, that was certain. And she wouldn't want Kylie to be a part of Lucas's life. So, just how far would Cordelia go to prevent something like that from happening?

Kylie wasn't sure, but she intended to find out.

Chapter Seven

As a general rule, Lucas usually avoided hospitals and doctors' offices. The sterile smell and the white-jacketed doctors just didn't set well with him. It was a childhood trauma association thing. Too many broken bones, bruised ribs and stitches from trying to play rodeo.

Yet, here he was inside his second medical facility in less than twenty-four hours. This one, the Brighton Medical Center, was about twenty times the size of Finn's clinic, and despite its back-to-nature claim, it was crammed with lots of those white jackets, sterile smells and patients. In this case, the patients were dozens of pregnant women.

One of whom was Kylie.

"I really have to go to the bathroom," she complained to Finn. She was wearing a dull gray-blue paper hospital-type gown while reclining on an examining table, and her stomach was bare. Well, it was bare except for some clear gooey stuff that Finn had smeared all over it moments earlier.

"Sorry," Finn apologized to Kylie. "You'll have to wait a few minutes before you can go. A full bladder helps with the ultrasound."

Lucas figured there was a thorough explanation for that, but he didn't really want to hear it. All he wanted was for the test to be completed and for Kylie and the baby to get a clean bill of health.

Until they'd arrived at the medical center, Lucas hadn't realized just how concerned he was that the kidnappers' drug might have harmed the child. In the past twelve hours, he'd had the case, Kylie and even Cordelia's brief but irritating visit to take his mind off such things. But those distractions didn't work now.

He needed to know if this baby was okay.

Finn held up a small device. "This is a transducer," he explained and began to move it over Kylie's goo-slick stomach. "It'll transmit the images so we can see what the little tyke is doing in there."

Kylie began to hum. Softly. Lucas wasn't sure, but he thought it was "Peter Cottontail." With the absurdly cheerful Easter notes coming from her closed mouth, she kept her attention fastened to the small, grainy screen. He divided his focus between it and her.

She was nervous. The humming proved that. Not that Lucas needed such an obvious clue. After what had happened to her, any expectant mother would have been worried about the test results. As an expectant father, he was certainly worried.

In addition to the nervousness and the humming,

Kylie looked exhausted. And probably was. The confrontation with Cordelia certainly hadn't helped, either. Why of all days had his former sister-in-law chosen this morning to drop by for a visit? It had been weeks, if not months, since Cordelia had come out to the ranch. Lucas didn't have the answer as to why she'd shown up out of the blue, but because he didn't believe in coincidences, he had a really bad feeling in the pit of his stomach.

Was Cordelia up to something?

And why hadn't she reacted to Kylie's clothes? After all, it appeared as if Kylie had just climbed out of his bed. Even more, why hadn't Cordelia said something about the pregnancy? Cordelia knew about the surrogacy, of course. In fact, she'd even volunteered to help Lucas decorate the nursery. She couldn't have known that Kylie was that surrogate, but why wouldn't Cordelia at least have shown some interest, or even displeasure, in the fact that Kylie was pregnant? That revelation had certainly hit him like a sucker punch to the solar plexus.

"Just to let you know, I plan to send the ultrasound to your doctor in San Antonio," Finn continued, moving the transducer to the side of Kylie's stomach. "But so far, everything looks good. The placenta's attached normally and the heartbeat looks good. The baby's active, has two arms, two legs. If you want to see them, just look here."

Finn used his index finger to trace parts of the fuzzy

image on the screen, but Lucas couldn't make heads or tails of it.

Apparently, Kylie was having the same problem because she glanced at Lucas and questioningly lifted her right eyebrow. They both seemed frozen in the moment.

They shared a smile. A brief one. It was laced with relief, fatigue and other emotions that probably only parents experienced. But it was still a smile. A reminder for him that Kylie and he had something in common, whether he wanted that or not. And suddenly that didn't seem as disastrous as it had the night before.

Oh, man.

He was so in trouble here.

Lucas didn't want his feelings toward Kylie to soften. He really didn't. But how the heck could he stop that from happening? And why did stopping it suddenly seem like a really stupid idea, anyway? After all, it was his baby, but she was the one carrying it. It just wasn't a good idea for them to be at odds.

Kylie flexed her eyebrows as if she understood the battle he was having. It was ironic. He now shared a camaraderie with Kylie Monroe. Worse, it wasn't simply camaraderie.

There was an attraction simmering between them.

Lucas mentally paused and waited for lightning to strike him where he stood. No lightning bolt. No cosmic rift. Just a moment of truth.

However, that moment of truth and admission didn't mean he would act on that attraction. No way. It would be a massive mistake. Because Kylie and he would never be able to get past what had happened to Marissa.

He mentally paused again.

Would they?

"How about the sex?" Finn asked, jarring Lucas out of his conflicted thoughts.

Since Lucas was staring right at Kylie, he saw the bittersweet reaction register in her eyes. Lucas knew there was emotion in his, as well.

She pulled in a slow breath, shook her head, moistened her lips. "I don't want to know, but you can tell Lucas."

She was obviously trying to distance herself from the baby. *Trying* being the operative word. And that led Lucas to yet another concern in his ever-growing list of concerns. This was his baby, yes, he didn't doubt that. But even though Kylie had said she would give him the child and leave, would she?

Would Kylie just leave?

"All right, we're finished," Finn announced.

He didn't have to tell Kylie twice. She barreled off the table as much as a pregnant woman could and headed straight for the adjoining bathroom.

"So, you want to know if you're having a little cowboy or a cowgirl?" Finn asked.

Of course, he was curious. Okay, more than curious. Since he'd found out that his surrogate was pregnant, he had formed mental pictures of both a son and a daughter. He had to adjust those images now that he knew Kylie was the mother. He'd always thought of his child as having dark hair. Like his. But there was a possibility that he or she would be blond.

With Kylie's blue eyes.

Fate and DNA certainly had a twisted sense of humor. Here he'd spent years despising those eyes, yet he might spend the rest of his life looking at them on a son or daughter whom he dearly loved.

"Well?" Finn prompted. "You want to know the gender?"

Lucas shook his head. "No." He wanted to get a few things straightened out in his life so he'd have time to savor the news.

Finn actually seemed disappointed. "Still having trouble coming to terms with all that's happened?"

Lucas sank down onto the chair tucked in the corner. "I'm having trouble with a lot of things."

"Hmm." Finn dropped down on the examining table directly across from him. "Buttin' my nose in here, but when's the last time you were with a woman? And I don't mean that in a general sense. I mean clothing removal, et cetera, et cetera."

It was sad, but Lucas it took him a while to come up with an answer. "About six months."

Finn stared at him.

"All right, almost a year." And it had been just sex. Comfort sex at that, with an old high school friend who'd been in town to visit her folks. Lucas couldn't even remember if it involved total clothing removal.

Heck, he couldn't remember if it'd been marginally satisfying. What he could remember was that he'd felt guilty as hell afterward. It'd been like cheating on Marissa.

"There. You have the answer to some of those things that are troubling you," Finn concluded. "Maybe you've never noticed, but Kylie's an attractive woman—"

"I was married, not dead," Lucas pointed out. "I'm a man, not a eunuch. I noticed."

Finn opened his mouth, probably to continue to plead his case as to why Lucas should have yet another round of guilt-producing sex, but thankfully Lucas's cell phone rang. Saved by the bell.

"Lucas Creed," he answered, dodging Finn's disapproving you-won't-get-off-that-easy gaze.

"It's Sheriff Knight. I've been working on those things we discussed, and we got lucky. Well, in one way. In another way, our luck just didn't hold out."

"Start with the good," Lucas requested. Maybe by then, he'd be in the right frame of mind to hear the bad. God. He really didn't need any more bad news.

"I called the detective in SAPD that you suggested, and he managed to locate a Tiffany Smith through her cell phone records."

If this were true, they had gotten more than just lucky. They'd gotten a huge break. "You're sure she's the right one? There's probably more than one person with that name in a city of over a million people."

"She's barely eighteen, a runaway. She recently had a baby, and she used that same surrogacy clinic you mentioned that your friend had used. With that kind of bio, I'd say she's the right one. I managed to talk to her, briefly, on her cell phone. She wouldn't tell me where she was. Fact is, she sounded a little scared. But she did agree to a meeting with you, me or both. Tomorrow afternoon, four o'clock, at Mama's Pizzeria on Broadway. You know the place?"

"I'll find it," Lucas assured him. Because this was too important a meeting to pass up. Since he didn't figure he would get the truth from Isaac Dupont, maybe Tiffany Smith had info or even evidence that could link Dupont to illegal surrogacy.

And to the kidnapping attempt on Kylie.

If that attempt had been made to silence Kylie, then Dupont was at the top of his list of suspects. He was also at the top of the list of people who riled Lucas the most. He didn't intend to let Dupont or anyone else get away with what had happened to Kylie.

"I did a little checking into the surrogacy clinic itself," Sheriff Knight continued. "It's just a suggestion, but you might want to take a hard look at the clinic's director, Kendrick Windham."

Lucas knew the name. It'd come up in his preliminary research. "I planned to do that just as soon as I'm finished here."

He'd read back through Kylie's now infamous article after she'd gone to bed, and even though she hadn't actually mentioned Kendrick Windham, it's possible that Windham thought she was referring to him. Or maybe he thought she was alluding to his highly successful clinic.

Alluding.

There was that word again. Kylie was right. All that sidestepping might have gotten her into a lot of trouble. Now, it was his job to end the trouble so she could concentrate on a safe and healthy pregnancy.

"Are you ready for that bad news now?" Sheriff Knight asked.

At the same moment the sheriff said that, Kylie came out of the bathroom. Lucas listened to what his fellow police officer had to say, and at the end of the explanation, he concurred. It was bad news.

Now he had to figure out what to do about it.

"Is everything okay?" Kylie asked.

Lucas nodded. That nod, though, was a huge lie. Things were far from being okay, but he'd save that for later. First, he wanted to try to sort through the implications of what he'd learned and then try to come up with a solution or two.

If that were possible.

She'd changed out of the paper gown and back into her maternity jeans and a loose tropical blue sweater that was almost a perfect match for her eyes. She glanced at both Finn and him, as if she were trying to figure out what they'd discussed.

"I'm outta here," Finn announced. He snagged his

jacket from the chair and headed for the door. "I'll let you know as soon as I get the results from the lab work. But I wouldn't worry. Everything looks good."

Kylie nodded and thanked him. However, as soon as Finn had made his exit, she turned her gaze on Lucas.

"I didn't ask about the baby's gender," Lucas volunteered, putting on his coat.

Shoot. She looked disappointed, as well. Lucas preempted that look by telling her what he'd just learned. "Sheriff Knight over in Gold Creek made some calls for me. He found Tiffany Smith."

"You're kidding." Kylie slipped on her own coat. "How?"

"We got some help from SAPD. They checked cell phone accounts. Anyway, Tiffany's agreed to meet with me tomorrow afternoon."

She cocked her head to the side, studied him. "If you managed to put all of this together, you didn't get any sleep last night, did you?"

"Not much." But then, she probably hadn't either. He opened the door to get her moving, and she fell into step beside him as they headed down a massive, glossy tiled hall. "I also want to do some checking on the clinic director."

"Kendrick Windham," Kylie provided. "I met him briefly. You?"

"Never saw him. I dealt only with the intake coordinator for the paperwork and the lab tech who processed my, uh, collection."

Sheesh. Why he'd nearly tripped over that word, he didn't know.

"You were lucky," Kylie concluded. "Windham apparently likes to meet all of his *girls* face-to-face. He's as slick as spit, if you ask me. He has Hannibal Lecter eyes. Come to think of it, he has a Lecter smile too. Seriously creepy. Definitely the kind of person you don't want to cross paths with unless you have no choice."

Great. Lucas had used a clinic with a slick-as-spit director. And because he'd used said clinic, that meant Kylie had used it, as well.

Nothing like a little extra guilt to bear.

"Okay, spill it. Is there something wrong with the baby?" Kylie demanded. Not only did she demand. She came to a complete stop just inside the exit.

"No. The baby's fine. You heard Finn say so."

Judging from her expression, she obviously wasn't convinced.

"Then what's wrong?" Her voice softened. "And please don't tell me all is well, because I know from your body language that it isn't."

He hadn't realized he'd been that obvious. Still, he hadn't intended to keep it a secret, especially since it involved her. Lucas drew in a long breath before he started. "I requested that SAPD provide protective custody for you. Sheriff Knight checked on it, but they told him they'd turned it down."

"Yes." She nodded. "The kidnapping attempt wasn't within their jurisdiction. And let me guess—they don't have the manpower or the funds to assist. Not until they officially open the case against Dupont." She pulled in a hard breath. "But not to worry. I can make other arrangements—"

"What other arrangements?" Lucas glanced at her and then out into the massive parking lot.

She obviously noticed that parking lot glance because she looked out the double glass doors, as well. She no doubt noted the parked vehicles just as he'd just done. Once a cop, always a cop.

"I can stay with my cousin in Houston," she suggested.

"Delmon," Lucas said. He knew him. Had grown up with him. And trusted him, for the most part. But there was a problem. "Don't know if you've spoken to him recently, but he seems to be out of town. I tried to call him this morning. Got his machine. I tried again while you were getting ready for the ultrasound. Still no answer."

Kylie shrugged. "All right. So, if I can't get in touch with Delmon, I'll hire a bodyguard."

That nonchalant shrug didn't fool him one bit. "You could do that, yes. It'd take time to find someone reliable. Days, maybe. And even then, you might learn the hard way that this employee isn't so good at stopping determined kidnappers."

Her shrug turned to a huff. "This isn't your problem, Lucas. You have enough to deal with already, and believe it or not, there are some things I can do for myself."

"Why did you tell me that you were my surrogate?" He didn't wait for her to answer. "Presumably, it wasn't because you wanted to make a get-it-off-your-chest confession. And I don't think it was part of chloroform haze, either. It's because you were scared. *Are* scared," he corrected.

Her chin came up, and he saw the fight brewing in her blue eyes.

Lucas cut her off at the pass. "You did the right thing by telling me. I know that. *Now.* If you hadn't, and if something had gone wrong, I never would have forgiven myself."

"Or me."

He couldn't argue with that. After all, he'd managed to hang on to his anger, hurt and blame for a long time. He was still holding on to it. But he couldn't let that get in the way now.

His child needed him.

"This isn't about forgiveness or blame," he insisted. "For better or worse, you're carrying my baby. And that baby is the most important thing. I won't let your pride or your fear get in the way of what has to be done. Because you see, Kylie, no one wants to protect this baby more than I do. *No one.* I'm willing to put my life on the line. You think a bodyguard for hire will do that?"

She blinked. "Kevin Costner did for Whitney Houston in that movie, *The Bodyguard.*"

His first reaction was frustration because she seemed to be trying to brush him off. But the frustration quickly passed when he looked at her. And then he remembered. When she had been his deputy, Kylie had always been the one to infuse a little humor into a bad situation. Even if that humor was a smoke screen to hide her own concerns.

"So, your answer is yes?" he asked. "You'll let me provide protection?"

"No."

He tried very hard not to groan, but gave up. "No?"

"No," she repeated. "Lucas, think this through. You can barely stand to be in the same room with me. Now you're saying we should stay together, under the same roof. *Indefinitely.*"

He really didn't like it all spelled out that way, but even the bare facts wouldn't make him back down. Not on this. "Temporarily," he added.

"*Temporarily* won't lessen the discomfort you'll feel when you have to face me every morning."

It wasn't exactly the facing that concerned him most. The danger was his first concern, but he couldn't dismiss this sizzling attraction, either.

A burst of winter wind came right at them when they stepped out of the building. Because they had a long walk through the massive parking lot, Lucas pulled the sides of his jacket tighter around him. It didn't help; the cold got through anyway. Ditto for the jeans. They weren't much of a barrier against the unusually bitter weather. He suddenly wished that he'd asked Kylie to wait inside while he brought his truck around to the front.

Kylie struggled with her own tan wool coat, but no matter how she shifted it, there wasn't enough fabric to cover her stomach. Lucas finally just reached out, hauled her against him and pulled her into the cover of his buckskin jacket.

"Thanks," she mumbled. Then, she started to hum. He couldn't help it. He smiled. He wanted to tell her that the closeness made him as uncomfortable as it was obviously making her, but it wasn't necessary. Kylie no doubt knew.

The cold and the moisture in the air had scabbed the surface of the parking lot with thin patches of ice. It was a reminder that the drive back wouldn't be easy on several counts. Still, he'd gotten her to agree to the protective custody. Now, they just somehow had to survive it.

Kylie stopped and glanced over her shoulder. Lucas turned, as well, and spotted what had captured her attention. It wasn't difficult to spot—a dark blue SUV entering the parking lot.

There were at least two dozen cars in the parking lot, and not all were stationary. Two were driving slowly toward the exit. Another was in the process of parking. However, the SUV seemed to stick out.

Lucas glanced at his own truck. It was still a good twenty feet away. He considered latching onto Kylie and running toward it for cover. But Kylie probably wasn't in the best condition for a run, and besides, there was no indication that they needed cover.

Well, no indication except for that tightening feeling in his gut.

"Is everything okay?" Kylie asked. But it didn't sound nearly so much a question as it did a concern.

Without taking his attention off the approaching vehicle, Lucas stepped to her side. He didn't stop there. He positioned himself slightly in front of Kylie and eased his right hand over his gun.

Just in case.

The SUV came around the corner just ahead of them. The driver must have stomped on the accelerator because the vehicle lurched forward and swerved. Not in the opposite direction, either.

It charged right toward them.

Chapter Eight

Kylie saw the vehicle and reacted.

But not as quickly as Lucas did.

Yelling for her to get down, he hooked his arm around her waist, and he shoved her out of the path of the oncoming vehicle. He twisted his body to take the brunt of the fall, and they landed on a narrow gravel easement just in front of a parked car.

It wasn't a second too soon.

The SUV sliced across the path where they'd just been standing. The vehicle clipped the shoulder of the parking lot and narrowly missed the car directly in front of them.

Fear slammed through her. God, what was happening? First, the kidnapping attempt, and now this. It couldn't be a coincidence.

Lucas drew his weapon, turned again and angled his body over hers, sheltering her. She cursed. So did he. This day had doled out enough without adding a near-death experience to it. And there was no mistake about it—they'd just come close to dying.

Kylie frantically dug through her purse, the one she'd picked up at her house earlier, and she pulled out her snub-nosed revolver as well. She didn't make a habit of carrying a concealed weapon, but after what had happened the night before, she'd wanted to bring the weapon with her.

Just in case.

Well, *just in case* had happened.

The SUV screeched to a halt, and Lucas dragged himself off the easement. Kylie tried to get up, as well, but he merely forced her back down.

"Stay put," he warned. "You can't put yourself in danger. Think of the baby."

Until he added that last part, she'd been ready to disagree. He was right. However, it sent her adrenaline and fear levels soaring. Finn had just given her a clean bill of health, and the baby was right back in danger again.

When was this going to stop?

Because she had no choice, Kylie did as Lucas said. But while taking cover behind the parked car, she repositioned herself so she could assist and return fire if necessary.

The SUV had come to a stop at the far end of the parking lot. She couldn't see anything behind the heavily tinted windows, but Kylie had no trouble hearing the driver of the vehicle hit the accelerator. The SUV lurched forward, and the back tires fishtailed on the icy surface of the parking lot. It sped away, leaving behind a cloud of exhaust.

That speedy exit got Lucas moving away from the

meager shelter of the easement. He kept his Glock ready and aimed, and he darted out into the parking lot.

"Did you get the license plate numbers?" he called out to her.

"No. You?"

He cursed again. Obviously he hadn't seen the license plate, either. Like the other vehicle that had followed her from San Antonio, this one appeared to have mud or something on the plates.

Without taking his attention off the exit path, Lucas took out his cell phone and used his thumb to stab in some numbers. Probably to SAPD. But that might not do any good. They were outside city limits. Again, out of SAPD's jurisdiction. But this latest incident might be enough to get them to open the investigation into Isaac Dupont's alleged illegal activity.

However, the question was, would that help? Or would it make things worse? She didn't think Dupont was the sort of man merely to accept an investigation without causing some waves of his own.

And that made her furious.

Because Dupont, or whoever was doing this, was putting Lucas's child at risk.

With her heart banging in her chest, Kylie stood, and her gaze whipped across the parking lot, first to one end, then the other. She didn't stop there. She studied the rural highway that fronted the clinic. No sign of the SUV. It, and its lethal driver, had simply vanished.

"Let's go after the SOB," she insisted, already storming toward Lucas's truck. "I think he turned left when he headed out of the parking lot. That means he's driving east."

Lucas did some storming of his own, and he easily caught up with her. He grabbed her arm, not delicately, either, and gently but firmly pushed her to the side of another car.

"You're not going anywhere. At least not until the police arrive. And even then, you're not going after that SUV, understand?"

She wanted to argue. Mercy, did she want to argue. Kylie wanted to lash out. To scream. "That driver could have killed us," she pointed out.

"Yeah. Believe me, I know. And that's the reason you're not going anywhere near him or her."

The anger and the frustration nearly got the best of her. She kicked not one rock but two. It didn't help. But that was a lot to ask of mere rock kicking.

"The cops should be here soon," Lucas told her. He got her moving back toward the clinic. "I want you to wait inside."

Inside. Where it was presumably safe.

Well, *safer* anyway. Maybe there was no place where the baby and she would be truly safe. A disturbing realization. One that hit her almost as hard as the fear, the adrenaline and the anger. And it made her understand just how little control she had in all of this. But she did have some control, and it was time for her to use it.

"I'll do it," she heard herself say.

Probably because he was surveying the parking lot and because he was thinking about that SUV, he tossed her a puzzled glance. "You'll do what?"

She said the words quickly, before she could do something stupid and change her mind. "Accept your offer of protective custody."

With his breath still gusting, he nodded. "Good."

Not exactly the word she would have used. More like *excruciating*.

"That SUV helped make up your mind, huh?" Lucas asked.

"That, and you pulled a Kevin Costner. You put your life on the line. For the baby," she quickly added.

He made a sound that could have meant anything. Kylie understood that ambivalence. On the one hand, staying with Lucas would make her feel safer. As safe as she could feel under the circumstances, anyway. But on the other hand, it would make her feel…

That was it.

The end of the sentence.

Staying with Lucas, being around him, would make her *feel*. And Kylie was positive neither of them would care for the outcome of that.

LUCAS TIGHTENED the last screw that held the tiny security alarm to the living room window. He immediately tested the device, nodding at the shrill, piercing noise before he turned it off and activated it. Hopefully, it would be sufficient to alert them if anyone tried to break into the house through this particular window.

He grabbed his tool box and went down the hall to tackle the last room. Along the way, he stopped to check on Kylie, who was installing the same type of security devices on the windows in the guest room.

She obviously didn't see or hear him because while she worked, she danced to the beat of the music coming through the tiny green headphones of the portable CD player she had clipped to the waist of her pants. For a pregnant woman, she certainly had some agile, almost seductive moves. Like a belly dancer.

Okay.

So, maybe that belly dancer part was his imagination—which seemed to be active lately.

Since they'd returned from the clinic, she'd changed her clothes because the others had gotten dirty in the fall onto the easement. She now wore gray pants and an emerald green shirt. Not some formless baggy outfit, either. The clothes clung to her, including her pregnant belly. Which for some men might have been a turnoff.

For him, it had the opposite effect.

It was as if his body seemed to know that her stomach carried his own precious cargo. That in turn became some kind of weird aphrodisiac.

And that made him one sick puppy.

Perhaps sensing he was there, gawking at her, she glanced over her shoulder and stopped swaying. With a screwdriver still in her hand, she pulled off her head-phones.

"Success. I think," Kylie volunteered. As he'd done, she tested the security alarm when she'd finished the in-stallation, and the sound momentarily stabbed through the room. "Yep. It works."

Though she quickly turned off the alarm, she didn't take her attention away from the window. Lucas fol-lowed her gaze. It wasn't on the window itself, but rather outside.

"Anything wrong?" Alarmed, Lucas practically dropped the toolbox, drew his gun from his shoulder holster and hurried across the room.

"Finn just dropped off his two Dobermans," Kylie informed him.

Lucas confirmed that when he spotted Finn by the barn. And, yep, there were the Dobermans, complete with what appeared to be a sack with a month's worth of premium dog food and two equally premium stain-less steel food bowls. Except these bowls were more the size of radial tires.

Lending his pets was a huge sacrifice for Finn, since Lucas knew his friend treated the two canines, Sherlock and Watson, like pampered children. It would be a sac-rifice for the dogs, as well, because they'd be sleeping in the barn and not inside Finn's sprawling house on the edge of town.

"I can't believe you're doing this. You don't even like those dogs," Kylie pointed out.

It was true. They snarled and growled at him any time Lucas got within ten feet of them. But hopefully they'd react the same way if an intruder approached.

"It's temporary," Lucas explained, aware that he was using that word a lot lately. Kylie's protective custody was *temporary*. The security alarms on the windows were *temporary*. Now, he only hoped his lust for his houseguest fell into that same *temporary* category.

Finn waved and climbed back into his car. Lucas re-holstered his Glock and went to retrieve his toolbox. One room to go, and then the house would be secured. Well, as secure as he could make it. Now, he had to hope that it was enough.

He opened the door to what he'd once called the "spare room," and he heard Kylie padding along behind him. Padding, because she'd removed her shoes and was now wearing a pair of thick gray socks. He debated whether he should just close the door and create some kind of diversion so she wouldn't see what was inside. But he debated too long.

"Oh," Kylie said, looking over his shoulder. "This is the nursery." She made the comment sound cheery enough, but it didn't fool him. Seeing this had to be difficult for her. A reminder of what would happen after she gave birth—when she would no longer be in the picture.

"You chose a good room," she continued. She brushed past him so she could enter. "It's right next to yours so you can hear the baby when he or she cries."

She pointed to the shrub-like tree just outside the window. "That mountain laurel is beautiful when it blooms. All those fragrant purple flowers. The baby will love that."

Her gaze eased over the crib that was still in its box. Ditto for the changing table. The only functional piece of furniture was his grandmother's rocking chair. She ran her fingers over the chair arm and gave it a gentle push so that it rocked slightly.

"I can install this last security alarm myself," he told her. And to prove it, and so they could hurry up and get out of there, Lucas got to work on the window.

"You still have a lot to do in this room. To get it ready, I mean."

"Yeah." He almost left it at that, but he didn't want her to get the wrong idea—that he was dreading the preparations for the baby or that the preparations weren't a priority. They were. "The intake counselor at the clinic told me that, uh, it was best if I waited until closer to the delivery date."

In case something went wrong with the pregnancy. Ironic. Because a lot was going wrong.

She sank into the chair and began to rock. "You know I want to go with you tomorrow for that meeting with Tiffany Smith."

"I know. That doesn't mean it's going to happen." He figured Kylie wouldn't let things end there.

She didn't.

"Tiffany is my informant, Lucas."

It was a good argument, but it wouldn't work. "And you think this somehow negates the fact that you'd be in danger if you go to a meeting in a public place with an informant you're not even sure you can trust?" Satisfied that he'd delivered the best argument he could, and equally satisfied that he hadn't convinced Kylie—he turned on his electric screwdriver to secure the alarm in place.

She waited until the whirring noise of the screwdriver had stopped before she continued. "I think my presence at that meeting might encourage Tiffany to talk. After all, she didn't have any trouble chatting up a storm when we met at the surrogacy clinic. She might not be so willing to tell you things that she'd tell me."

Lucas gave her a flat look. "Nice try. Not gonna work, though."

Kylie returned that look. "We could bring one of the deputies or maybe Sheriff Knight with us. For extra protection. That way, I'd be safe."

"Sheriff Knight's going with me, since he's the one who made contact with Ms. Smith." Lucas engaged the alarm and stooped down to put the screwdriver back in the toolbox. "One of the deputies is staying here with you, while the other mans the office. See? Everything's taken care of, so there's no need for you to try to work things out."

The rocking stopped, and Kylie eased up from the chair. He could see the battle brewing in her eyes. "And at no point during your planning did you think to discuss this with me?"

Lucas tapped his chin and pretended to think about it. "No. Because I never had any intention of letting you go to that meeting."

"I'm a trained law enforcement officer," she quickly pointed out.

"You're pregnant."

That earned him a glare and a really loud huff. "Last I heard, pregnancy and PMS don't affect a woman's aim."

"Oh, no. You're not going to drag me into a male-female argument. This isn't about your gender. It's about your being more vulnerable." He turned, planning to make a hasty exit, but she caught onto his arm and pulled him back around.

Not the best idea she'd ever had. Lucas would bet the ranch on it.

Because lately, anytime they touched, sparks flew. Heck, who was he kidding? Every time they breathed, they created not just sparks but flames.

"The sooner we get to the bottom of what's happening, the sooner this case will be closed, and the sooner I'll be less vulnerable," Kylie said. There was a slight quiver in her voice, proving his theory about sparks and flames. "And the sooner this case is closed, the sooner I can leave your protective custody."

She was right on the money. But for some reason, that last part didn't sit well with him. Maybe because he was no longer anxious for her to leave. Or maybe because he was aroused beyond belief just by being this close to her.

Or maybe it was because he was just an idiot.

"Our living arrangements are getting to you already?" he asked.

"Of course. And it's not a guess that it's getting to you, as well."

He saw her pulse on her neck pick up speed. Like her voice, it was practically trembling. Strange, because Kylie usually wasn't the trembling sort, and that little tremble fascinated him. He frowned, rethought that. Lately, everything about her fascinated him.

The part of his brain that was still functioning logically knew nothing good could come of this attraction. Nothing good other than great sex, anyway. Which suddenly felt much more important than the nothing-good-could-come-of-this part.

He changed his mind a couple of times about what to say. "You look…"

"Best not to finish that," she interrupted.

Yeah. But he finished it anyway. "Interested."

"Interested?" she repeated. "That's an *interesting* word."

Lucas pushed for an answer. "Are you?"

She made a vague motion toward the door, as if she were indicating that she was about to leave. But she didn't leave. Instead, she huffed, an indication that she didn't have any more willpower than he did. "I'm human."

It was an odd response. Well, odd if he hadn't seen the underlying response in her expression. Yes, she was human. So, was he. And Lucas had never been more aware of that than he was now.

She angled her head slightly. Studied him. Her hair shifted, sliding over her neck and the top of her shoulder. If she'd looked even a little bit frightened, he would have stepped back. But that wasn't an expression of fear.

It was something much more dangerous.

"You look…" But she didn't finish.

Lucas supplied the answer that was already on the tip of his tongue. "Interested?"

She shook her head and mumbled some profanity. "Hot. Really, really hot."

He almost laughed. And he tried to force his mouth to stay closed so he wouldn't say something stupid like, "Kiss me." Or, "Have sex with me." In fact, his mouth was suddenly thinking of all kinds of inappropriate suggestions.

"You look really, really hot to me, too," he confessed.

She stiffened a little, as if surprised. "Strange."

"Why?"

"Because it's not hot in here."

He lifted an eyebrow. "Oh yes, it is."

Her mouth quivered, threatening to smile. Lucas could feel his own mouth doing the same. But while this little mouth conflict and word war were somewhat amusing, the rest of him felt anything but amused.

He felt…ready.

And she obviously sensed that readiness. Her gaze

eased to his. Eye contact. And she held his gaze for several seconds before hers slid over his body.

"I think I might be trying to figure out what to do with you," she admitted.

The blood rushed to his head. And to other parts of him. "You *think?*"

"Okay. I *know* I'm trying to figure it out. Trust me, anything we figure out together right now would be a mistake," Kylie whispered, her voice laced with frustration. "You'd regret it. *I'd* regret it."

He couldn't disagree with any of that. In addition, Lucas thought of plenty of reasons why he should back away. The danger. The uncertainty. Their past.

None of those things stopped him.

Before he could talk himself out of it, Lucas reached out and did the very thing he'd believed he would never do. He curved his hand around the back of her neck and hauled Kylie to him. Against him. Pressed her breasts against his chest.

The battle continued.

She looked up at him. Moistened her lips. Probably not a come-on, but it had that effect on him. Of course, at this point anything except a no would have been a come-on.

Breath met breath. And he caught her scent. Something warm, inviting and feminine. It fired his blood and sent his body into a claim-and-possess mode. Even then, he could have stopped.

But he didn't.

Instead, he leaned in and braced himself. Lucas soon realized he couldn't possibly have braced himself enough.

He took her mouth as if he owned it. The taste of her exploded through him. It was a taste he hadn't even known he'd craved until now. And he was certain that one taste wouldn't be nearly enough. Oh, man.

Her touch didn't help things, either. She slid her fingers along his biceps. A sensual, slow caress. And that wasn't all. Moving, she brushed her hip against the front of his pants. Yep. There it was. The striking match. It revved his body up another notch—as if he needed any such enticement. Kylie alone was all the enticement he needed.

He roughly caught her hair with one hand, kept the other on the back of her neck and drew her tightly against him. Until he could feel every silky soft inch of her. Including her stomach.

His lips pressed hard against hers. Taking. Not a soft gentle kiss of comfort, either. There was no comfort in the sensual moves of their mouths. This was all white-hot heat, fueled by raw emotion.

He suddenly wanted more. A lot more. Kylie obviously did, too. She fell into the rhythm of the kiss. And into the rhythm of their bodies as they adjusted. Fighting to get closer. Needing each other in only a way that lovers could need each other.

She slid her leg along the outside of his. Lucas upped the ante. He locked onto the back of her knee and positioned it so that it hugged his hip. It brought the centers of their bodies into as much direct contact as they could have, given that she was pregnant. She was soft in every place that he was hard. And that made them the perfect fit.

Lucas moved against her as she moved against him. The kiss didn't stop. Nothing stopped. Except maybe his breath. But he didn't care if he ever drew breath again. Suddenly, this seemed to be everything he had ever wanted.

And that was exactly why it had to stop.

He repeated that. Twice. It still took every ounce of his willpower to do what he knew he had to do. He couldn't let this lead to sex. He just couldn't.

"There," he said forcing himself away from her.

"There," she repeated. She sounded as if she'd just completed a marathon. Fast breath. Equally fast pulse. And she had a wild, unfocused—and yes, aroused— look about her.

"Does that prove I'm human, too?" he asked.

"No." She pulled in several quick breaths. "It just proves we're both *interested*. And stupid."

Man, was she ever right. That interest was testing the limits of his jeans. And with the flames still burning through him, Lucas desperately wanted to reach out and pull her back into his arms. If he pushed it, just a little, it would lead to sex.

And even through the lust haze, he knew that would be a really bad idea.

Lucas forced himself to consider the consequences. They could dismiss a kiss, but sex was a whole different matter. Sex with Kylie would change everything. As it was, they had a thin, tenuous agreement: protective custody for the sake of the baby. Sex would rock that agreement to the core and confuse and distract them at a time when they needed no more confusion, no more distractions.

She turned away from him and focused her attention on the picture of the crib that was pasted on the front of the huge box. "This pregnancy really has my hormones going crazy."

Lucas considered that a moment. "That's what you think the kiss was about—pregnancy hormones?"

"Yes." But she didn't sound as if she believed it any more than he did. "That, and I've always been a little attracted to you."

He couldn't totally suppress that idiotic sound of surprise that escaped his mouth. "*You* were attracted to *me?*"

"Definitely."

"You're kidding."

"No. In fact, one summer when Marissa and I were fifteen or so, we watched Finn and you skinny-dip at Palmer's Creek."

Lucas shook his head. "You did what?"

"Yeah, well, I'm not exactly proud of it, but it's what estrogen and other raging hormones do to a young woman's body. Don't worry. I averted my eyes before

I could get a glimpse of full frontal nudity." She shrugged. "But I did get a mental glimpse of full adolescent lust."

Still not understanding this, he leaned closer to make sure there was no humor in her eyes. There wasn't. "Lust for me?" he clarified.

"For you. But when I saw how Marissa reacted—I'm talking she had the serious hots for you—I told my body to look elsewhere."

It was as if he'd just been given a rewritten version of the history of his life. For one thing, he hadn't even known Marissa had been interested in him until well after high school. And he'd never noticed Kylie looking at him with anything other than friendly interest. And all of this new information made him wonder—what would he have done if he'd known? Would Kylie and he have somehow found their way to each other? The attraction was certainly there.

The phone rang, interrupting Lucas's unwanted trip down memory lane. Because there wasn't a phone in the nursery, he went back down the hall to the kitchen.

"Lucas Creed," he answered.

"Sgt. Katelyn O'Malley, SAPD."

Lucas didn't recognize the caller, but he did recognize that tone. A cop's tone for official business. Any levity and lust he was feeling evaporated.

"Are you the officer investigating the incident in the birthing center parking lot?" Lucas asked.

"Not exactly. But I think our cases might overlap. I

spoke to the detective that you and Sheriff Knight have been dealing with. I understand you're to meet with Tiffany Smith tomorrow afternoon?"

"That's the plan."

"Well, I think you'll have to change your plans. Ms. Smith was brought into the E.R. at Southeast Hospital about an hour ago."

Hell. "What happened?"

"Car accident. Or maybe not an accident. We're waiting on the tox results and some other tests. Looks like there's forced trauma. This might even have been an attempted homicide."

Why hadn't he seen this coming? *Why?* The moment Sheriff Knight had located the young woman, they should have somehow made her tell them where she was so they could provide her with protection.

"Tiffany Smith is in and out of consciousness, but she's asking to speak to you, Sheriff Creed. And she also wants to see someone I believe you know—Kylie Monroe."

That last request didn't do much to steady Lucas's nerves. Oh, man. What was going on?

"Ms. Smith says it's critical that she see you and Ms. Monroe immediately. A life-and-death matter, she says," Sgt. O'Malley continued. "My advice? Get here soon, because it's life-and-death for her, too. The doctors aren't sure she'll last through the night."

Chapter Nine

Kylie listened as Lucas finished his phone call. It was the third he'd made since they'd started the forty-five minute drive from the ranch to the Southeast Hospital in San Antonio. The first call had been to his deputy, Will Trapani, who, judging from the one side of the conversation that she had overheard, was still sick with the flu, suffering from chills, fever and other assorted cruddy symptoms.

Will's description of his ailments had created some get-well, sympathetic remarks from Lucas, but he'd cursed when he'd hung up. Obviously, he'd counted on having the deputy as backup. He couldn't very well call out his other deputy, Mark Jensen, because that would essentially leave Fall Creek without any police protection.

Will's flu bug had precipitated a second call to Sheriff Knight, who apparently was planning to meet Lucas and her at the hospital. That was a security measure that Kylie understood because, after all, Knight was a lawman. What she didn't understand was Lucas's third call. To Finn. Lucas asked him to go to the hospital, as well.

"Please don't tell me you expect Finn to be able to return fire if we get into a situation while we're visiting Tiffany Smith?" she asked.

"I'd rather arm his Dobermans. I've seen Finn shoot, or rather attempt to shoot, and it wasn't a pretty sight." Lucas slipped his phone back into his pocket. "If there's medical red tape, I want Finn to cut through it for us. I don't want you in that hospital any longer than necessary."

The concern for her safety was loud and clear. And Kylie greatly appreciated it, too. It wasn't a question of bravery but rather one of survival. If she got hurt, or worse, so would the baby.

But she had to wonder if Lucas's concern had increased because of that hot kissing session?

Kylie wanted to dismiss what'd happened. Mainly, because it was easier to dismiss it than to try to figure out the consequences.

And there would be consequences.

No doubt about it. Lucas was probably already feeling massive amounts of remorse. Ditto for her. In her mind, he was still Marissa's husband. Except she darn sure hadn't been thinking about Marissa when she had been kissing him.

That didn't lessen the guilt.

In fact, it made it worse.

It was scary that something like physical attraction

could temporarily cause them to push aside all those barriers that they'd spent three years erecting. Part of her wanted those barriers back. It was safer that way. But she couldn't deny that Lucas's kisses had awakened feelings inside her that she thought she would never have. Not for him. Not for any man.

Kylie pondered that a moment.

And since it seemed too overwhelming and totally unsolvable, she decided to continue to blame it on the pregnancy hormones. Those little suckers had gotten a lot of playing time lately, and she would continue to give them a little more.

"I should have insisted Tiffany Smith go into protective custody," Lucas mumbled.

It wasn't his first such mumbling, either. It was the fourth time he'd said something similar since he'd gotten the call from Sgt. O'Malley at SAPD.

"My guess is Tiffany wouldn't have told you where she was," Kylie informed him. "After what she's been through, I doubt she's the trusting type."

"I should have pressed her to tell me."

"And the pressing would have sent her straight into hiding. You said Sheriff Knight thought she sounded afraid. Well, there you go. She wouldn't have simply put her safety into the hands of strangers."

Apparently her attempt at reassurance meant nothing because Lucas only grumbled again. Kylie totally understood. Yet another form of guilt, but guilt all the same. It was becoming her forte. She didn't need to tell him that it would be a while, maybe forever, before the guilt would go away.

"Stay right next to me," Lucas instructed as he stopped his truck in the parking lot of the hospital. "And don't make me regret bringing you along."

As if he'd had a choice about that. Tiffany had apparently made it clear to Sgt. O'Malley that she wanted to speak to both Lucas and her. Kylie could only hope the young woman had information that would stop the kidnappers from coming after her again. Of course, Tiffany could have paid a very high price for simply having that information.

This might even have been an attempted homicide. Lucas had told her that's what Sgt. O'Malley had relayed to him.

Kylie hated to jump to conclusions because this could have been a botched carjacking or even a bad case of road rage. She prayed that's all there was to it. While she was at it, she added a prayer for the young woman. Tiffany didn't deserve this.

They entered through the emergency room, and after Lucas spoke briefly with the nurse at the check-in desk, they were directed to a tall, brunette doctor who was in the nearby hallway. Kylie glanced around and didn't see either Finn or Sheriff Knight. She also adjusted her purse, in case she needed to get her weapon in a hurry. The hospital appeared safe enough, but she wasn't about to risk their lives on that appearance.

When they approached the doctor, Lucas pulled back

his jacket so she could see the badge clipped to his belt. "I'm Sheriff Lucas Creed. This is Kylie Monroe. We're here to see Tiffany Smith."

The doctor wore a nametag that identified her as Shelby Morgan, M.D. She motioned for them to follow her deeper into the hallway so they weren't right next to the other E.R. patients. "I'm sorry, but you might have made this trip for nothing. Ms. Smith isn't allowed visitors. She lapsed into a coma about fifteen minutes ago."

Kylie's heart sank. Mercy, it was awful news. "Do you think she'll regain consciousness soon?"

"Hard to say. She has some frontal lobe damage, along with some internal injuries from the accident. It also appears she recently had a difficult childbirth. She has some untreated complications from a botched episiotomy, among other things. She has an infection, a serious one, and that'll only impede her recovery. *If* there is a recovery."

Kylie's heart sank even further, and any glimmer of hope sank right along with it. "You don't expect her to make it?" she asked.

The doctor shook her head. "The prognosis isn't good. We're trying to locate her family now, but she didn't give us much information to go on."

"Tell me about this car accident," Lucas insisted. The emotion had cooled his voice, but Kylie knew that coolness wasn't indicative of the frustration, concern and even the anger he was feeling. "What happened?"

"The other sheriff already asked me that."

"Sheriff Knight?" Kylie questioned.

"Yes. He arrived just as Ms. Smith went into the coma. He's outside her hospital room. Standing guard, along with the other officer from SAPD." She paused, studied them with weary eyes. "I suppose the security's necessary?"

"Could be," Lucas answered. "It'd help to know what happened to cause the accident."

"We don't know much. According to the officer who brought her in, it appears that Ms. Smith was driving in her vehicle when she was run off the road. Her car nose-dived into the Basse Street basin. Ms. Smith couldn't or wouldn't say much, but she did tell us…" The doctor looked down at the sheet of notebook paper she held in her hand. "I'm more or less quoting here, 'I shouldn't have talked to Kylie Monroe. It's all a terrible mistake.'"

Because she needed it, Kylie leaned against the wall. "Someone wanted to silence her before she could say anything else to us."

"That terrible mistake part could refer to the car accident," Lucas pointed out.

Or maybe Tiffany had meant her conversation at the surrogacy clinic. Had she told someone about that conversation? Or had someone forced her to tell them after the article Kylie had written had been published?

Either way, they were back to square one.

No doubt that article had probably put Tiffany in the hospital. In the end, it might cost the young woman her life.

"I'll check on Ms. Smith's tox screens," Dr. Morgan

informed them, heading down the hall toward the elevator. "I'll let you know what I find out. Oh, and I'll tell Sheriff Knight that you're here."

"Hell," Lucas said under his breath when the doctor walked away.

Kylie totally agreed with the sentiment. Tiffany's life was hanging by a thread, and there was nothing they could do about it. Worse, they didn't seem to be any closer to identifying the culprit.

"This is all my fault," Lucas grumbled. "It shouldn't have happened."

"Funny, I was thinking the same thing. That article—"

"I'm the one who didn't provide a potential informant with adequate protection. That's standard law enforcement procedure, and I blew it."

"Tiffany wouldn't have needed protection if I hadn't written that article."

He stared at her. "Are we vying for some blame championship?"

"No." Kylie blew out a long breath. "I think we're tied for that honor."

Kylie automatically reached out to him. Touched his arm with her fingertips and rubbed lightly. Subconsciously she'd probably meant it to be a comforting gesture, but it suddenly seemed too intimate.

She expected Lucas to back away, both mentally and physically. She also expected herself to back away.

But they stayed put.

Not only that, he reached and caught her shoulders.

He looked straight into her eyes. "I'm not going to let them hurt this baby, understand? I'll do everything within my power to protect you."

It was a convincing promise. And it didn't seem to matter that he had no way to back it up. Kylie believed him. Maybe because she *wanted* to believe him.

She groaned softly, and she was the one to back away. Until all of this had started, she'd managed to suppress her feelings for the baby. Oh, not totally. But she'd certainly been able to make it through an hour or two not thinking about all the things she'd miss by cutting herself out of the baby's life.

Lucas's adamant, heartfelt promise melted away all that suppression.

"We should have never kissed," she told him. "It was a mistake, and it changed things that shouldn't have been changed."

He shook his head. "It didn't feel like a mistake."

"That's why it was one." She groaned. "Lucas, it's going to be hard enough for me to give up this baby. I can't—"

Kylie stopped herself, before she could say something they'd both regret. And they would regret it. Because if she were to fall hard for Lucas, then leaving both him and the baby would be next to impossible.

She *had* to leave.

Though Lucas had kissed her, held her and had just sworn to protect her at all costs, he couldn't give himself to her. And she couldn't try to make a relationship work when she knew in her heart that such a relationship would only cause him more pain.

He rolled his shoulders as if trying to work out the fatigue and frustration. "I don't want to feel this way. But I can't help myself."

Kylie nodded. "I understand. Because when you see me, you'll always think about Marissa."

His gaze came to hers. "That's the problem, Kylie. When I see you now, I see *you.* The mother of my child. A woman. And it's tearing me apart inside."

Kylie's mouth dropped open. "Are you saying—"

"I'm saying that I can't," he interrupted. With that, he walked a few steps away.

She understood that, as well. It encompassed a lot. Their past. Their present.

And, no doubt, their future, too.

"I need to concentrate on the case," she heard him say. "I can't let my personal feelings get in the way here. It'll only cause me to lose focus. And if I lose focus, the baby could be hurt."

"All right," she said tentatively.

Not because she disagreed. She didn't. But the problem was how to make themselves focus when they were going through an emotional upheaval. However, Lucas soon proved he hadn't just made the comment off the cuff. He truly intended to take action.

When he pulled his phone from his pocket, she walked closer until they were side by side. "Who are you calling?" Kylie asked, alarmed.

"SAPD. I want to make sure they keep a guard posted outside Tiffany's door. Then, I'm calling directory assistance—so I can get the number for Kendrick Windham, the director of the surrogacy clinic. I want to speak to him."

Kylie hadn't seen that last one coming. It seemed an almost desperate act. Of course, they were desperate. Lives on the line and all of that. "You think talking to Windham will actually do any good?"

"Probably not. But I want to hear his reaction when he learns that Tiffany Smith is in the hospital. And that she's still alive."

"Alive, *barely,*" Kylie pointed out. "And in a coma with a serious infection."

"But Windham doesn't know that."

Kylie considered that, and didn't like where her consideration took her. "A game of cat and mouse," she mumbled as Lucas made the calls.

When she had been in law enforcement, she'd played a few of those games herself, but she had to wonder who the mouse was in this situation. Did Windham even have a part in any of this? It was a question she couldn't answer. Especially since her mind kept going back to Cordelia and the hatred she'd seen in the woman's eyes. If Cordelia had somehow found out about the secret surrogacy, then maybe she would have been desperate enough to stop it.

But that seemed a stretch, even for Cordelia.

"Windham didn't answer," Lucas explained, walking back toward her. "I left a message with his answering service."

Kylie didn't like the sound of that. "Dare I ask what you said in that message?"

"I simply told him what had happened and that I wanted answers about Tiffany Smith."

Well, that would certainly stir up a hornets' nest. Because even if Windham hadn't had anything to do with Tiffany's accident, he still had to address the questions of why he'd used an underage surrogate. And why she'd obviously received such shoddy medical care during and after delivery.

"I understand you're accusing me of a felony or two," she heard someone say.

She turned toward the man's voice. So did Lucas. She saw an imposing, dark-haired man making a beeline toward them. He was about six feet tall and wearing perfectly tailored khakis, a cream-colored pullover sweater and an expensive calf-length black cashmere coat. An eraser-size icy diamond winked in his left earlobe.

His stride was confident. Cocky, even. The stride, posture and attire of a man who was accustomed to getting everything he wanted.

"Now, would you care to make those accusations to my face?" he asked. He didn't ask it in a friendly sort of way, either. "Oh, in case you don't recognize me, I'm the lawyer you've been maligning—Isaac Dupont."

WELL, THIS AFTERNOON was just full of surprises.

Bad ones.

Lucas figured the man walking toward them would top the list of bad surprises.

"Sheriff Creed, I presume," Isaac Dupont said.

Since it wasn't exactly a question, Lucas didn't answer. But he did glare. He couldn't help himself. He disliked the man on sight. However, he had to admit his judgment might be clouded by the kidnapping attempt, the godawful experience in the parking lot of the birthing center and Tiffany Smith's "car accident." It was difficult to think highly of a man who might have been responsible for all those things.

Lucas stepped in front of Kylie and hoped like the devil that she stayed put so he could give her some shred of protection.

"I'll make those accusations," Lucas volunteered. "I'll add a few more if you'd like. And I have no problem doing that to your face."

Kylie tapped him on the shoulder and shot him a warning glance.

Which he ignored.

"What are you doing here?" Lucas asked Dupont.

"I heard the infamous journalist, Kylie Monroe, was in the building." It sounded as if he'd rehearsed his answer, or at least had given it plenty of thought. "I decided I'd pay her a little visit."

"Heard?" Lucas questioned.

Dupont bobbed his head. "Yes. It's a past tense verb. But I don't suppose a cowboy-cop like you from Hickville would recognize a grammatical part of speech when you hear it."

"You'd be surprised at what I know." Lucas leaned in, violating his personal space. "And I don't have any trouble recognizing a smart-ass suspect who's trying to avoid answering a simple question. In my experience, the main reason suspects do that is because they're guilty."

"So, now I'm a suspect?" If that bothered him in the least, Dupont didn't show it.

"Puh-leeeze," Kylie interjected. "You didn't know we were suspicious of you? Then, you're either an idiot or a liar. Maybe both."

Lucas looked at Kylie and made sure he put a little badass spin on it. He wanted answers from Dupont, but he didn't want Kylie's antagonism to rile the man to the point of attempted murder. She must have gotten the point, finally, because she stepped back.

One battle down.

Another to go.

"Why are you really here?" Lucas demanded of Dupont.

"As I said, I came for a little visit. And a little warning. You can write your tabloid trash stories all you want, Ms. Monroe, but leave me out of them. I'm a respected attorney in this city, and I won't have my name dragged through your own personal version of mud."

Lucas shrugged. "She never mentioned your name. Guilty conscience, perhaps?"

Dupont met him eye to eye. "Let's just say I'm intuitive."

"Or maybe you're just paranoid," Lucas offered. "I hear there are medications for that."

Oh. There it was. A flash of anger that went bone-deep. The cool facade stayed in place, for the most part, but Dupont couldn't quite keep the emotion out of his gray-blue eyes.

"Why don't you explain what part you played in providing surrogates to Kendrick Windham's clinic?" Lucas demanded. "I'm especially interested in those who are underage and medically unqualified."

"I don't have to answer that. I don't even have to be polite to you." To Lucas, that sounded very much like a threat. "You have no jurisdiction here, cowboy."

"No," Lucas enunciated the single word carefully while trying to put a choke hold on his temper. While he was at it, he caught Kylie's arm and moved her back even farther away from Dupont.

It didn't stop her.

"But FYI, Sheriff Creed does have lots of friends in SAPD," Kylie pointed out. "Oh, and he also has a loaded .40-caliber Glock in the shoulder holster beneath his left arm."

Amused, or least trying to appear amused, Dupont flexed his eyebrows. "Am I being charged with something?"

"Maybe loitering," Lucas suggested. "Threatening a police officer? Being a general nuisance?"

"You could never make those charges stick."

"No. But it could land you in lockup for a few hours while SAPD takes their time processing the paperwork."

Dupont exaggerated a noisy yawn. "Bored now. Good afternoon, Sheriff Creed, Ms. Monroe. I trust this isn't the end of our *dispute*. I'll be in touch. But remember what I said—keep my name and any reference to me out of your so-called articles."

He turned, and it was then that Lucas saw the other person approaching them. Not Dr. Morgan. The guy was dressed in drab gray sweats, a hoodie and running shoes. His salt-and-pepper hair was damp, as if he'd just finished a workout.

And he wasn't alone.

He was walking side by side with Finn.

Lucas automatically drew his weapon, holding it close to his thigh so that it wouldn't be so conspicuous to the patients and staff but so he could use it if required.

"Well, well. The gang's all here," Dupont said, stopping. He looked back at Lucas and grinned from ear to ear—especially when he noticed the unholstered Glock. "In case you don't recognize your latest visitor, that's—"

"Kendrick Windham," Kylie supplied. Because her arm was against his, Lucas felt her muscles tighten.

"I finally made it here," Finn announced. "And I ran into an old acquaintance in the parking lot."

"You know each other?" Lucas asked.

"We attended the same conference a few years ago." Finn looked at her. "What's going on?"

"It's a long story."

"I don't have time for long stories," Windham interjected. "My answering service called, said you left a message. Something about a former client who's been hospitalized?"

Unlike Dupont, Windham's comment didn't seem threatening. In fact, nothing about him seemed threatening.

Well, except those eyes.

"Why don't you test the waters with him, Sheriff Creed?" Dupont suggested, adding a tsk-tsk. "An experiment of sorts. Accuse Kendrick Windham of a felony or two." Dupont paused for a heartbeat and aimed another of those oily grins at Kylie, then at Lucas. "He's not a forgiving kind of man, the way I am. It'd be interesting to see just how fast he kills you."

Chapter Ten

Kylie had met Kendrick Windham for a few short moments nearly six months ago, but it'd been more than enough for her to form an unfavourable opinion of him. That opinion didn't change as he stood in front of Lucas and her, seemingly sizing them up just as they were him.

"See you later," Dupont said, still smiling. Not exactly subtle like Windham. Dupont simply didn't seem to care if anyone thought he was guilty of a crime. Probably because of his old money and business connections, he thought he was above the law. Maybe Lucas and she could use that arrogance to nail the guy.

Well, if Dupont was guilty, that is.

Suspect number two, Kendrick Windham, had just as much motive to silence her as Dupont had. Maybe more. Because, after all, she could directly link him to the clinic and to Tiffany Smith.

"How is Ms. Smith?" Windham asked.

"Alive," Lucas answered, reholstering his Glock.

Kylie watched Windham's expression. If he was afraid that Tiffany might rat him out for illegal surrogacy or even kidnapping and attempted murder, he wasn't showing it. Yep. Definitely slick. It made her think of pathological liars, serial killers and other unsavory sorts. Someone with that kind of personality could definitely try to kill anyone who threatened to expose his dirty dealings. And that's exactly what she'd done in a roundabout way with that article.

"Let me do some checking," Finn volunteered. "I'll see if I can find out how Ms. Smith is doing."

The moment Finn stepped away, Windham checked the budget-draining gold watch that glimmered on his left wrist. "I can't stay long. Appointments. And I obviously have to shower and change. I just popped by on my way home from the gym so I could wish Ms. Smith a speedy recovery."

"She's not allowed visitors," Kylie informed him.

"Too bad. I might be able to cheer her up. The few times I saw her, we got along quite well."

"Did you now?" Lucas asked skeptically.

Windham spared Lucas an inquisitive glance. "We got along well in the sense of a clinic director and a client. Definitely nothing to cross ethical boundaries. And certainly nothing personal." Another check of his watch. "When she's allowed visitors, perhaps you can give me a call. I'd like to let her know that I'm here for her."

His inflection didn't change, but that sent a chill snaking down Kylie's spine. If Tiffany did regain consciousness, there was no way Kylie would deliver what could easily be a veiled threat. In fact, Lucas and she would make sure SAPD had Tiffany's room well guarded.

"If you really want to help Tiffany, you could always offer to pay her medical bills," Lucas suggested. "I'm sure she doesn't have insurance, and her injuries have been complicated by an infection from poor medical care during her delivery."

"I'm afraid that's out of the question, especially since her injuries resulted from a car accident. I phoned the hospital on the way over, asked a doctor friend who works here to give me an update on Ms. Smith's condition," he said in response to Kylie's suspicious look. "Imagine if I reimbursed all or even a few of my clients for services not directly related to their surrogacy agreements. I'd be bankrupt. I'm not in business to go bankrupt."

"And the bottom line for you is money?" Kylie asked.

"Of course." He drew in an impatient breath and tossed a glance Lucas's way. "Phone me if her condition changes. You obviously know the number."

With that, Kendrick Windham turned and briskly walked away.

"What was the heck was that visit all about?" Kylie mumbled.

"Marking his territory, I'd say." Lucas paused. "You think Dupont and he orchestrated this tag team visit, or was it coincidence they showed up here at the hospital at almost the same time?"

"Well, you don't believe in coincidences, so I know where you stand on the issue. Still, I'm not so sure what's going on with those two."

And that bugged her. A lot. Had they indeed arranged the simultaneous visits, or had someone else alerted both of them? After all, she hadn't gotten a good look at either kidnapper. Neither Windham nor Dupont matched the sketchy physical descriptions of the would-be kidnappers, but maybe one or both of the suspects were here at the hospital. Watching Tiffany to make sure she didn't say anything incriminating.

That theory sent her gaze rifling around the nearby waiting room and the curtained examination stations. She studied each person, letting her anxiety nearly get the best of her. She pulled back and tried to see the hospital through normal eyes. Everything seemed, well, normal.

But that didn't mean it was.

"Sheriff Knight won't let anyone into Tiffany's room who doesn't belong there," Lucas said.

Her gaze came back to his, and she saw that he was examining her with those cop's eyes. Not that she was difficult to read. Especially not for him. Lucas seemed to be very good at knowing her every emotion.

"So, which one do you suspect?" Lucas asked. "Dupont or Windham?"

"Both," she answered honestly. "But I don't think they're partners."

He made a sound of agreement. "Neither of them are

partner material. Too self-obsessed. But I'm willing to bet either could really be into criminal intent—especially when there's money to be made."

Yes. But which one? Kylie hoped they learned that before the kidnappers decided to strike again.

Finn rounded the corner of the hall, fast. Before he could reach them, Kylie knew from his dour expression that something was wrong.

"What happened?" Kylie asked, dreading his answer.

"Tiffany Smith regained consciousness—"

"I need to see her," Lucas insisted.

When Lucas started to walk away, Finn caught his arm. "She was only awake a few seconds before she went into cardiac arrest."

The news sucked the breath from Kylie's lungs. She dropped back, leaning against Lucas, allowing him to support her. "She's dead?" Kylie mumbled.

"Yes. Dr. Morgan did everything she could to save her," Finn added solemnly. "But Ms. Smith's injuries were just too severe for her to survive."

Lucas cursed, scrubbed his hands over his face and cursed some more. He pounded his fist against the wall. Kylie pulled him back before he could hurt himself.

"Mind filling me in as to what this Attila the Hun reaction is all about?" Finn asked. "Because you didn't tell me much when you called and asked me to come to the hospital."

Kylie tried to answer and realized she needed breath to do that. Hers hadn't fully returned yet.

Lucas didn't answer right away either, though he seemed to be breathing. Angry, rough gusts of air came from his mouth. "Tiffany Smith was a surrogate at the same clinic that Kylie used. Kendrick Windham's clinic. Tiffany might have had information about those men who tried to kidnap Kylie."

"Wait a minute!" Finn's eyes widened, and he snapped his fingers. "She said something right before she died."

"What?" Kylie and Lucas asked in unison.

"I didn't hear. But I'm pretty sure Dr. Morgan did."

Lucas broke away from Kylie and Finn's grip and practically sprinted down the hall.

Kylie was right behind him.

Chapter Eleven

Lucas didn't think he'd ever felt more exhausted, confused…or frustrated. Tiffany's words kept replaying in his head. It had been relentless for nearly half an hour now, during the entire drive back to the ranch, and it just wouldn't quit.

One word at a time.

Like jabs from a switchblade.

They probably had that effect on him because they weren't just words. But a warning. Tiffany had apparently used her dying breath to make sure she didn't take that warning to the grave.

They'll do whatever it takes to stop Kylie Monroe and Sheriff Creed.

Too bad Tiffany hadn't identified who *they* were. Perhaps because she didn't know. Maybe she, too, had been threatened by the two ski-mask-wearing kidnappers. Maybe she'd eluded them, temporarily, only to have them run her off the road and into that basin.

They'll do whatever it takes…

Lucas hadn't exactly needed Tiffany's warning to tell him that. But it had been chilling to hear the doctor recount it verbatim. Because before Tiffany's deathbed warning, he'd been able to hope that the men had merely wanted to kidnap Kylie. Of course, that in itself was a serious enough crime. Serious, but not necessarily fatal. But if Tiffany was right, the stakes were much higher now.

Life and death.

The slight popping sound drew Lucas out of his mental word war, and he glanced at Kylie. Seated next to him, one foot tucked beneath her, she'd just blown a bubble from her strawberry-scented chewing gum. That cheery scent had permeated the entire cab of the truck. And Lucas actually welcomed it.

Actually, he welcomed *her* company.

As bad as all of this was, it felt good to have someone to share it with. Even if he would have given his right arm to make sure Kylie and the baby stayed safe.

He didn't understand this change of heart he'd had toward her. And he didn't want to question it either. Maybe the bone-weary fatigue was part of that. Lucas didn't want to question that, either. He simply wanted to accept this truce, temporary or not, between them.

Of course, there was the other thing that had settled between them. And it wasn't peaceful. It was fiery, turbulent and wrong. Yet, he didn't think he had a snowball's chance in hell of fighting it.

For whatever reason, his body had decided that it

wanted Kylie. And his brain was going right along with that decision.

"They killed Tiffany because she learned something," Kylie said. Another bubble. Another soft pop. "Or maybe she knew nothing, but they thought she did."

Lucas had already gone down that road, and it led him to yet more guilt and frustration. If the kidnappers had somehow heard about Tiffany's plans to meet with Sheriff Knight and him, then that alone might have given the SOBs motive to kill her. It also might have given them a motive to kill Kylie and him, as well. Perhaps even Sheriff Knight, who would surely be watching his back.

"This isn't your fault," Lucas said, because he knew what Kylie was thinking.

"It is. Let's face it. I should wear some kind of warning sign around my neck so people won't get too close. I'm one of those crud magnets."

"No. You're a journalist, apparently a very good one, who wrote an article that hit some nerves."

"And got a woman killed."

"Don't go there, Kylie. You were a cop long enough to know that sometimes bad things just happen."

She glanced at him, as if she were trying to look into his heart.

Were they talking about Marissa now or Tiffany?

Lucas wasn't sure of the answer. But he was certain that all this stress and worry couldn't be good for Kylie or the baby.

She shook her head. "But something about what happened to Tiffany doesn't feel right," Kylie added. "You know what I mean?"

He was with her on that point, as well. Something just didn't fit, but Lucas couldn't quite put his finger on what that was. But then, lately a lot of things hadn't fit.

"A car accident's risky," Kylie continued. It didn't surprise Lucas that she was voicing the same concerns that were inside his head. Kylie and he had always worked well together as sheriff and deputy. "Why not just wait until she got to her destination to kill her? It didn't appear that she was driving in the direction of police headquarters. More in the direction of the interstate.

"If they'd waited until she was somewhere more private, they could have made sure she was dead. Left no loose ends. Perhaps even made it look like a real accident. After all, she was sick. How hard would it have been to incapacitate a sick woman?"

Both stayed quiet a moment. Thinking. Trying to make the pieces of the puzzle fit.

"So, where does that take us?" she asked. "This was perhaps a crime of opportunity? Maybe not even connected to the illegal surrogacy activity? In fact, this could have been some kind of grandstanding fiasco meant to make Dupont or Windham look very guilty."

He thought of Cordelia.

Lucas figured Kylie did, too.

And then he immediately thought of Kylie.

It was as if he had attention deficit disorder. Too many thoughts. Too many distractions. Too little focus. Or better yet—the wrong kind of focus. Yeah. There was definitely nothing semipeaceful about this whirlwind that had taken over his brain.

There was only one thing that should be on his mind: catching the kidnappers and their boss so he could ensure Kylie's safety. That was it. Nothing more.

But, of course, knowing that didn't make it so.

So many feelings were going through him. All the unresolved pain from Marissa's death. The need to protect Kylie. Her scent. Yes, her scent—not the bubble gum, either—but something warm and inviting. The way she moved. The way she looked at him. This was definitely a male-female thing, and it was gaining momentum at an alarming speed. After all, even Tiffany Smith's death couldn't cool him down.

"You must be exhausted," he said, almost hoping that was true. "When we can get back to the ranch, I'll fix you something to eat, and then you can turn in early for the night."

She slid her hand over her stomach and rubbed in wide, gentle circles. "I don't think food will sit well with little Lucas here. Not to worry. Nothing serious. Just some indigestion."

That drew his attention to her belly, and he thought of a way he could take her mind off things. "You never did ask why I didn't have Finn 'fess up about the baby's gender."

"Yeah. Why didn't you?"

"It probably seems weird, but I wanted to keep it a surprise. At least for a little while longer, until things settle down."

She paused, nodded. "I understand that."

There. He saw it. Some of the tension drained from her eyes. Her stomach massage slowed. Her shoulders relaxed just a bit. It was enough encouragement for Lucas to continue.

"Can you imagine me being a father?" he asked.

"Of course." She said it as if jumping to his defense. "You'll be great. And I know you've always wanted kids."

That put a lump in his throat. But he pushed it and the thoughts of Marissa and their unborn child aside. There was nothing he could do to help them now, but he sure as heck could help Kylie and this baby.

"I've heard diapering can be tricky. I've signed up for a class," he shared with her.

"A class?" Her tongue went in her cheek. "Oh, to be a fly on the wall. The rough and rugged cowboy tackles a newborn and Huggies."

"There's a feeding and burping class, too."

Her lips quivered. "You're making that up."

"Scout's honor."

"You were never a Scout." She stared at him. "You smiled," she added.

"Did I?" But he was fully aware that he had. It seemed odd, as if it'd been so long since he'd given those particular facial muscles a workout that they actually felt stiff.

"There's hope for you yet, Lucas Creed."

He didn't know exactly what she was doing, but it was working. Here he'd been trying to cheer her up, but she was doing the same thing. Kylie was taking the weight of the world off his shoulders. And right now, there was an awful lot of weight on him.

He hadn't discussed his cases with Marissa. Though there'd been only a few serious crimes in Fall Creek, there had been a death resulting from a domestic dispute and several fatalities from car accidents. Early in their marriage, he'd brought up a detail or two of a case, but it had bothered Marissa to the point of giving her nightmares. He'd learned to leave his badge at the office.

Out of the corner of his eye, he watched as Kylie blew another bubble and then used her tongue to gather the pink gum back into her mouth. Despite the seriousness of their conversation, that caused him to do a double take. For such a simple, mundane thing, it seemed awfully erotic. It caused the blood to rush to his head. And to other parts of him.

Ah, sheesh.

Not this, not now.

She was exhausted. Had indigestion. Was just coming down from a terrible ordeal. He needed to think with his brain and not the brainless part of him below the waist.

"You're upset," she said. She put her gum into the foil

wrapper and discarded it in her purse. "Did you think of something we've missed?"

He almost asked why she thought that, but then Lucas followed her gaze to the death grip he had on his steering wheel. His knuckles were actually white.

In addition to attention deficit disorder, he was also wearing his heart on his sleeve.

Or rather, on his knuckles.

"It's nothing," he lied.

She stared at him. "You're sure?"

"I'm sure you don't want to know."

She waited a moment. "Oh."

Which meant she knew.

Another pause. "What if I confessed I feel it too?" she asked.

He mentally cursed. Great. Here they were up to their necks in danger, and he was getting an erection just thinking about her. "I'd tell you not to confess it."

"That won't make it go away."

"It's still better left unsaid."

"It could be a lot of things," Kylie said, obviously ignoring his not-to-confess response. "Self-imposed celibacy—"

"Has a short shelf life," he supplied.

She made a *hmm* sound, but it had just a tinge of amusement and frustration to it. "So, it could be just dark and primal animal urges."

He liked that term because it implied simple lust. But there was just one problem with labeling it simple lust—he'd lusted before. Plenty of times. But it hadn't felt like this. This was an overwhelming, consuming need that would probably drive him crazy.

Lucas came to a stop in front of the ranch, as close as he could to the front porch, and both of them just sat in silence for a few moments. Even though the sun was on the verge of setting, there was still plenty of light. He didn't let it give him a false sense of security. Nothing would after Tiffany's death.

He examined the perimeter of the house. Each sprawling live oak and pecan tree that dotted the landscape. Every shadow. Any place that a kidnapper might hide.

"I don't feel the compulsion to hum so I *think* all is well," Kylie mumbled. "How about you?"

He considered that. Considered that it was safer to be inside the house than sitting in his truck, where they were stationary targets. "Let's go."

The moment they stepped from the truck, the dogs came barreling out of the barn. With everything else going on, Lucas had somehow forgotten about Sherlock and Watson, Finn's prize Dobermans.

But he didn't forget them now.

Both came right at Kylie and him. Like oil-black streaks, complete with barking and snarling. The dogs skidded to a stop only a few yards away, but they didn't stop with their aggressive behavior.

Kylie moved closer to him, so that the side of her left breast brushed against his arm. She was the only spot of warmth in the chilly air.

"Sit!" Lucas ordered.

And much to his surprise, they obeyed. No tail-wagging or other friendly gestures, but the dogs didn't lunge after Kylie and Lucas when they stepped onto the porch, unlocked the door and went into the house. The newly installed security system immediately began to whine, and Lucas punched in the numbers on the keypad to temporarily disarm it. He rearmed it the moment they shut the door.

"Those Dobermans hate me," Lucas grumbled, tossing his keys onto the table in the entry.

"They hate everyone but Finn," Kylie pointed out. "They're cut-rate security, though."

"You haven't seen the price tag on that dog food he buys for them. It'd be cheaper to buy a side of prime beef."

Kylie smiled. Or rather attempted it. She did manage a nervous laugh, but there was no humor in it. "I lied about the humming. I did want to hum. But I really wanted to get inside."

"Yeah. I know."

She paused.

Kylie didn't have to say a word, but he knew what she was thinking. Their conversation about dark and primal urges had zapped both their bodies into a frenzy.

"We can resist this," he said.

Her eyebrow arched and Lucas shrugged.

He thought of plenty of reasons why he shouldn't pull her into his arms, why he should back away. The danger. His badge. The need for him to remain professional, objective and focused. They were all good solid reasons.

And yet none of them stopped him.

She looked up at him. But not just any ordinary look. *The* look. Her eyes were ripe with need for comfort. And more. Much more.

Her breath was already thin and fast. He saw the pulse jump on her throat. And that air just kept on sizzling. Lucas ignored every warning his body was sending him and gathered her into his arms.

But that wasn't all he did.

He leaned in, and his mouth claimed hers. The sensations slammed through him as the kiss intensified. Fast. Hard. Strong. Like a fist. Resisting wasn't possible. So he took everything she offered. *Everything.* And upped the stakes.

Grappling for position, she turned and shoved him against the door and went after his shirt. Fast and frantic. Like her breath. Like the hot, needy look in her eyes. It was a race. Against what, Lucas didn't know, but it didn't matter. All he knew was that they had to have each other now.

Kylie cursed when his coat wouldn't cooperate and when she encountered the shirt and its buttons underneath.

Lucas didn't help her. He was on his own mission. One that required the use of both hands. He seized the bottom of her sweater and shoved it up. The stretchable-waist pants went down, just beneath her belly. He found her panties. Cotton and lace. Not much of a barrier at all.

With his mouth on hers, Lucas slid his hand into that lacy barrier and found exactly what he wanted. *Her.* Hot and wet. Ready. He sank his fingers into her, sliding his thumb against the most sensitive part of her. And he went deeper. If they were going to cross these boundaries, he sure as hell intended to make it worth the ride.

He succeeded.

She made a sound. A rich, feminine moan of pleasure. Her eyelids fluttered down. She slid her leg along the outside of his. And she moved with him. Pushing against him. Sliding her hips forward. Moving in rhythm of the strokes of his fingers.

"You're going to have to do something about this," she insisted.

"I'm trying."

"The bed?" she managed. "The floor?"

It was tempting. He suddenly wanted her more than his next breath. But if he took her to bed, or to the floor, he wouldn't be able to think. And even though parts of him shouted that this wasn't a thinking kind of situation, it was. Kylie already had more than enough to deal with. In the past few days, she'd been through hell. So, while his body was yelling for him to take her right then, right there, Lucas knew that wasn't the right thing to do.

He continued the strokes of his fingers. Continued to push her to the edge.

"Why aren't we doing this together?" she asked.

But she didn't just ask. She reached for his zipper and hit pay dirt. She closed her hand over his erection and nearly had him jumping out of his jeans.

Once he got his eyes uncrossed, he caught her hand to stop her from fully unzipping him. "If you do that, I can't think."

"And that would be…bad?" She moaned and tossed her head back when his fingers went deeper inside her.

"That's it," he whispered. "That's the look I want to see."

"Really? This look?" She blinked, obviously trying to focus. "It can't be very attractive. I'm about to fall."

"No. You're beautiful, and you're about to fly. Fly for me, Kylie. Let me feel you when you fly."

She did. Lucas felt her body close around his fingers. Felt her soar until she reached a shattering climax.

And Lucas was right there to catch her.

He felt something brush against his arm and heard the crash. Even though her eyes were glazed from passion, he could see her fight through the haze to see what had happened. Lucas did the same.

His body went on full alert, and he reeled around. Searching for whatever had made that noise.

His first thought—and not a pleasant thought, either—was that there was an intruder in the house.

Chapter Twelve

Lucas reached for his gun, but Kylie saw him stop in mid-reach when he glanced down at the floor. She looked down, as well. There was the silver photo frame, the glass shattered.

Marissa's picture.

Kylie wanted to ask what had happened, how it'd gotten there, but she didn't have enough breath gathered to speak. So, she did a little mental detective work. She'd noticed Marissa's picture on top of the Mexican-tiled table in the foyer. Unfortunately, that table was right next to where Lucas and she had been groping each other. One of them had no doubt knocked it over.

Talk about a symbolic interruption.

Now that the wild passion had been sated and her body was returning to normal, Kylie quickly fixed her clothes so that she wouldn't be standing half-dressed in front of Lucas. Not that he would have noticed. He had his attention nailed to that picture.

Lucas stooped down, slowly, and in the same motion,

he slipped his gun back into his shoulder holster. He picked up the frame first, or rather what was left of it, since it was now disconnected. He touched it as if it were the most fragile, most precious thing on Earth.

Kylie felt the ache in her heart. Not just for Lucas and the guilt he was no doubt feeling. But the old guilt returning, as well.

Without looking at her, he reached up and put the picture itself into the table drawer and then began to retrieve the pieces. One by one. Again, slowly.

"It's just glass," he mumbled.

"Yes," she agreed because she didn't know what else to say. Glass. Something to protect the photograph. Too bad they didn't make some kind of protection for the human heart because Kylie was certain that her heart would be broken into a million pieces before this was over.

Lucas stood, disappeared into the kitchen, and she heard the sound of the glass being dumped into the garbage. She dreaded his return, dreaded what she would see in his eyes. Her blood pressure shot up when his footsteps grew closer, heralding his reentry into the foyer.

He stopped in the arched opening that divided the family-style kitchen from the living room and foyer.

"Thank you," he said.

Since her head was still fuzzy from the orgasm and the interruption, Kylie decided it was a good time to hush and let him finish. Because quite frankly, she didn't have a clue why he'd said that.

"I know how hard it was, *is*," he corrected, "for you to have this baby. Thank you."

Kylie couldn't stand the confusion any longer. "Did I miss something? One minute we're doing the whole dark and primal sex thing against the door. The picture falls. You pick up the glass. Take it to the kitchen. And… okay, here's where things really get confusing for me— you obviously have some kind of mental breakdown in there?"

The right corner of his mouth lifted. "No breakdown. I just came to my senses. I've been rude to you. Angry. And God knows how many mixed signals I've sent. I want to be honest with you, Kylie. I care for you."

Her heart soared.

"I really do care," he continued. He shifted. Not just his body. His gaze, too. "But I'm not sure I can ever get over what happened."

Her heart crashed.

And she silently cursed for allowing herself to believe, even for a few seconds.

Against her better judgment, she went to him. "Lucas, if you're worried about me falling apart after I have this baby, then don't. I'm a survivor. Have been since sixth grade, when my mom ran off to find herself and I moved in with Grandma Meg." She waved off the sympathetic look he gave her. "Don't pretend you don't know what I'm talking about. Because of Grandma Meg, I had to be a survivor because I was considered a flake by association."

He shook his head, obviously caught himself in what would be a polite but obvious white lie, and then shrugged. "Okay, you were the only student in any rural Texas high school to bring tofu pitas to school. And you wore sandals that had soles made from recycled tires."

Yes. She remembered those sandals. Comfortable but definitely not a positive fashion statement.

"I'll let you in on a secret, Lucas. I was torn between loving the only person who really loved me—Meg— and trying to live the life of a normal kid. I couldn't wait to shake off all those things that made me different from everyone else. I wanted to fit in. I wanted respect. That's why I became a deputy. It took me over a year of therapy to realize that, by the way. That's why I was working at Energizer Bunny speed while I wore that badge. The feet ahead of the brain."

Kylie paused and drew in a slow breath. "Funny though, after everything that happened, after I resigned, Grandma Meg's house was the only place I wanted to be. It was a sanctuary."

"And your prison," he promptly pointed out. "You cut yourself off from people, Kylie, especially the people you'd known since you were a kid."

"I couldn't face them. Couldn't face you." She made the mistake of facing him now. He was standing there, very much the cowboy in his jeans and white cotton shirt.

Mercy, the man had her hormonal number.

Here she was, reacting to him as if he hadn't just

minutes earlier given her the orgasm of her life. And he'd done that without even having sex with her. Leave it to Lucas to accomplish the impossible.

"So, where do we go from here?" she asked, not really expecting an answer. And she certainly didn't expect the answer that came from his sensual mouth, which she'd been admiring.

"Cold showers are out. They're useless. They just make you cold."

She laughed, until she realized there might be an underlying message there. "I have the same effect on you—I leave you cold."

"I wish."

He couldn't have shocked her more if he'd hauled her to the floor and had sex with her. "You're admitting that?"

He lifted his shoulder. "Seems pointless not to. I mean, after that whole dark and primal sex thing against the door."

Lucas was right. They'd been tiptoeing and lying to themselves. Well, at least she had. "I wish it was just lust," she mumbled.

"Me, too," he said after a moment.

All this honesty was really starting to get to her. "Sweet heaven, Lucas. What are we doing to each other? We're driving each other crazy, that's what. We really need to catch those kidnappers and their boss so all of this will end."

"And you think that will *end* it?"

Lucas reached out and pulled her to him, easing her into his warm embrace. Unlike before, this embrace wasn't fueled by passion. It probably would have been safer if it had. But while this wasn't safe, it was like coming home.

And Kylie wasn't exactly pleased about that.

Because this would end. The close quarters, the embraces, the kisses. The nonsexual orgasms. The poignant, heart-revealing moments.

It would end.

And like the broken glass from the picture, she'd be left with only the pieces. The Humpty Dumpy syndrome.

"You're thinking too much," Lucas said as he tightened his grip around her. He brushed a kiss on her forehead.

And that's how Cordelia found them when she unlocked the door, threw it open and stormed inside.

"WHAT THE HELL is going on here?" Cordelia demanded. Her hands went on her hips, and Lucas could see that the muscles in her face were so rigid that she looked as if she just had a massive injection of Botox.

Because their guest had tripped the security alarm when she had barged in, Lucas crossed the room and disengaged it to stop the noise.

"I can't believe what I'm seeing here." And just in case there was any doubt at to what she meant, Cordelia aimed a glare at Kylie.

"Well, you wouldn't have seen it if you'd knocked first," Lucas reminded her. He also did something he should have done months ago. He grabbed Cordelia's key ring and extracted the key to his house.

She grabbed his arm with a fierce grip when he tossed the key ring into her open purse and started to walk away. "Why are you doing this to Marissa?"

Oh, this was going to get messy.

But then, things often got that way with Cordelia. She was a messy, complicated person.

For years, Cordelia had resented Kylie's friendship with Marissa. But she hadn't resented it enough to try to build a relationship with her own sister. Cordelia was a scratch-the-surface, superficial kind of person who wasn't really into deep meaningful interactions. However, there were times, like now, when he saw genuine concern cloud her eyes.

Too bad her concern was misplaced.

"Kylie is in my protective custody," Lucas explained. Of course, that didn't explain the embrace or the flush still on Kylie's cheeks. Still, he didn't owe Cordelia that kind of explanation.

"I know about the baby," Cordelia announced.

Because that intrigued him, and because he thought it was a good precaution, Lucas repositioned himself between the two women. "And what do you think you know?" Lucas asked.

"That she's your surrogate. That the child she's carrying is yours."

Okay. So, her announcement no longer intrigued him, but it was a little alarming.

"And just how do you know that?" Lucas asked.

Kylie took his question one step further. "Better yet—*why* would you know?"

She spared Kylie another glare but addressed Lucas. "I was concerned. I wanted to make sure the clinic you used was reputable so I had Finn make a few calls—"

That had Kylie moving closer. "Finn?"

Cordelia paused and had that deer-caught-in-the-headlights look. "Yes. Because he's a doctor, I thought he could get answers faster than I could."

"And he got those answers," Kylie concluded, not sounding any happier about it than Lucas was.

Why hadn't his best friend mentioned any of this? It wasn't as if they hadn't seen each other. In fact, over the past forty-eight hours, he'd seen more of Finn than he had in a month. Finn had had plenty of opportunity to tell him.

"I went to the surrogacy clinic," Cordelia continued. "I met with the director, Mr. Windham. He tried to assure me that Kylie was a suitable surrogate. Obviously, he didn't know she's unfit to carry your child."

Lucas decided to inform her of a few conclusions of his own. "You're wrong. But let's assume for one minute that you're right. What am I supposed to do about it? The pregnancy's a done deal. The baby will be here in four and a half months. He or she isn't a toy I can exchange at Wal-Mart."

Cordelia had to get her teeth unclenched before she could speak. "Just because she conned her way into being your surrogate, it doesn't mean she has to be part of your life. You could order her out of your house. You could have her stay with someone else."

"I don't want her to stay with anyone else. I want Kylie right here." To prove his point, he hooked his arm around Kylie's waist and pulled her closer.

Kylie's glanced at him. She had that have-you-lost-your-mind? look on her face.

Cordelia reacted as if he'd slapped her. She actually pressed her hand to her heart and started to back away. "I won't let you do this. I won't let Kylie Monroe destroy your life the way she destroyed Marissa's."

"Well, that's not up to you, now is it?" Lucas hated to be cruel, but what he hated even more was Cordelia being cruel to Kylie.

Now, Cordelia turned her venomous gaze on Kylie. "If you continue to stay here and insinuate yourself into Lucas's life, I'll pursue legal action."

"For what?" Kylie asked. "Last I heard, it wasn't illegal for a grown woman to become a surrogate."

"I'll sue the sheriff's office for the wrongful death of my sister. I'll ask for millions, and I'll keep suing until I've bankrupted both of you and the entire town if necessary."

It was an anger-laden threat, but Lucas knew that didn't mean Cordelia wouldn't go through with it. If she did, it would hurt not only the sheriff's office, but it would also hurt Kylie. Still, there was no way he could back down now. Kylie was just starting to trust him. He was starting to trust her. There was a spark of life in him that he'd believed he would never feel again.

Kylie and the baby were responsible for that.

He wasn't going back to that dark, lonely place where he'd spent the past three years.

Lucas was on the verge of telling Cordelia a less emotional version of that when her cell phone rang. Still obviously steaming, she gave him a this-isn't-over huff and yanked the phone from her purse. He was close enough to see the caller ID information as it flashed onto the lighted screen.

Oh, hell.

That information set off all kinds of alarms in Lucas's head.

Lucas watched Cordelia carefully as she, too, glanced down at the caller ID. Turning away from them, she answered the call. She kept her responses whispered, simple and brief. *It's not a good time. No. No. Yes.*

"I have to go," Cordelia said abruptly. She dropped her phone back into her purse and went to the door. "Think about what I've said."

"Do I have to?" Lucas called out.

But he was talking to the air because Cordelia was already gone, leaving just a blast of arctic chill where she'd once been standing.

Lucas went to the door, as well, closed it, locked it and reset the security alarm.

"Cordelia knows Kendrick Windham, the surrogacy clinic director," he said, turning back to Kylie.

Kylie blinked. "What?"

"That call was from him. I saw his name and number on her caller ID."

Kylie shook her head. "You think he's the one who told her that I'm your surrogate?"

"Seems reasonable that the info would come from him. What isn't reasonable is that those two would feel the need to continue to stay in phone contact. Maybe Cordelia bribed him, and now he wants more money." But then something else came to mind. "Or maybe Finn's the one who did the bribing."

"I don't understand—why would Finn help Cordelia find out anything, especially about the baby? And why wouldn't he tell you about it?"

Both were darn good questions, and Lucas grabbed the phone and punched in Finn's number. Because it was time he had some answers.

"Talk to me about Cordelia," Lucas said the moment Finn answered.

"Well, good evening to you, too."

"Cordelia," Lucas prompted, ignoring his friend's sarcasm. "She was just here and said you'd helped her find out about Kylie being my surrogate."

"Hell's bells." Finn didn't stop there. He cursed some more, and it would have done a sailor proud. "Cordelia is a pain-in-the-butt-blabbermouth."

"That might be, but did you help her?"

"Only because she was relentless. She kept calling and kept dropping by the clinic to say how worried she was about you. She'd read Kylie's article, and she said she kept thinking that maybe the surrogacy was all a scam."

"Why would she care if it was?" Lucas asked.

"She didn't want you to get hurt."

Lucas played with that explanation a few seconds. It wasn't something he could totally discard. From time to time, Cordelia had tried to mother him.

When it suited her mood and motives.

"I made a few calls to the surrogacy clinic for her," Finn continued. "That's all. And it was just to give her peace of mind."

"It didn't work. Definitely no peace of mind."

"No. But then, I didn't know that Kylie was your surrogate. And I damn sure didn't know that Cordelia would be able to finagle that kind of information out of the clinic director." He paused. "Does Cordelia plan to cause trouble for you?"

"Seems that way." In fact, he could count on it. "I want the truth, Finn. Is there more to this than what Cordelia and you are saying?"

"What are you accusing me of?" Finn demanded.

"I don't know—yet."

But Lucas hung up the phone with an unsettling feeling in the pit of his stomach that something horrible had been set in motion and there was nothing he could do to stop it.

Chapter Thirteen

Something wasn't right.

That particular feeling had been with Kylie for nearly an hour now, and it just wouldn't go away. It was something raw and hot that churned her stomach. At first, she'd tried to dismiss it as indigestion brought on by Cordelia's visit and the homemade vegetable beef soup and buttery garlic bread that Lucas had fixed for dinner. But unfortunately, Kylie didn't think this uneasy feeling was related to food or Cordelia.

"Woman's intuition?" she mumbled under her breath. "Wild imagination?" She tried again. Grasping at straws. "Leftover orgasm adrenaline?"

Whatever it was, she obviously wasn't going to get much sleep tonight, so Kylie tossed back the log cabin quilt and reached for the pair of thick socks that she'd left next to the bed. She slipped them on, along with Lucas's bulky berry-red robe and started to pace across the hardwood floor.

However, she stopped momentarily when she got to

the window and decided it was a good idea to avoid openly pacing in front of it. There was a curtain, but she didn't want to risk that her shadow would fall against that curtain and give away her exact location.

Oh, great.

Now, she was bordering on paranoia. This certainly wasn't the quiet, serene pregnancy she'd dreamed of having. Of course, that's exactly what she had managed for four and a half months. Peace and quiet. Well, quiet anyway. It'd been three years since she'd had any real peace. And now things had heated up with the kidnappers, Tiffany's death and the way Lucas and she were carrying on in the lust department. Kylie hoped she didn't have to say which of those things surprised her the most.

Who was she kidding?

Lucas was the big surprise. He cared for her, he'd admitted. Yet, he'd also quickly added that it didn't matter, that it might lead to nothing. So Kylie did her best to rein in her feelings.

Even though she knew it was already too late.

Somewhere along the way, she'd started to fall pretty hard for Lucas Creed. But the real question was, what was she going to do about it?

She heard the slight cracking sound, and her pacing came to a dead stop. She lifted her head. Listened. Even though she didn't hear anything else, she retraced the sound and realized it'd come from outside.

Not that unusual, she reminded herself.

After all, the ranch was surrounded by woods. Lots of things could make cracking sounds in the night. Tree limbs stirring in the breeze. A coyote savaging for his dinner. Even Finn's dogs.

But her stomach churned even harder.

Keeping out of the direct line of visibility, Kylie eased toward the window and fingered back the edge of the ivory-colored cotton curtain. The moon was still relatively full, and the sky was clear. She could see a portion of the backyard and the barn.

No one was lurking out there.

No bad guys in ski masks.

Nothing.

That thought barely had time to settle in her mind when the door to her bedroom flew open. Kylie reached for her gun, which she'd put on the nightstand. But it was Lucas. He stood there with the golden light from the hall haloing behind him. He looked like the answer to a few raunchy fantasies she'd recently had.

He was armed and naked.

Well, almost naked, anyway. He wore only gray boxers that dipped below his navel.

Well below it.

No shirt. No shoes. Nothing to obstruct the rather nice view she had of his rather nice body. And what a view it was. He was solid. Not overly muscled. Not overly anything. A real man's body, with a toned stomach and a sprinkling of chest hair.

"Did you see anything?" he asked.

She was certain that she looked surprised. Because her mind was on, well, having sex with Lucas, it took her a moment to realize that wasn't a sexual kind of come-on look in his eyes. Those were cautious, vigilant eyes. Only then did Kylie remember she was in the process of peeking out the window. Plus, there'd been that little cracking sound she'd heard only moments earlier.

Oh, yes.

She wasn't having trouble keeping her priorities straight.

"All seems well out there," she reported, releasing the curtain so that it closed. That didn't ease his vigilant expression. "Is it?"

He shook his head. "I don't know. I heard something. A crunching sound."

Cracking. Crunching. Both synonyms for noises they shouldn't ignore, especially after everything that'd happened. "I heard something, too."

That was the only verification Lucas needed to get moving across the room toward her. First, he eased her away from the curtain and, while avoiding the window himself, he reached for the phone on the nightstand next to the guest bed.

"Stay down," he told her.

Kylie did. She grabbed the log cabin quilt and carried it to the corner near the closet. That new position took her out of the line of fire from both the window and the doorway. Just in case.

She listened as Lucas called Mark Jensen, his healthy deputy, and requested assistance. He hung up and made his way to her in a crouching position.

"You think it's necessary to bring Mark in on this?" Kylie asked.

"We need backup so that someone will be in here with you while the grounds are being checked."

"Good point." Kylie didn't consider it cowardly that she didn't want to be left alone, either. The pregnancy had made her vulnerable. Dying wasn't nearly as much of a fear as was having something happen to the baby.

She motioned toward his snug boxers. "Just a suggestion, but you might want to put something else on before Mark gets here. Appearances and all that."

He glanced down at his lack of clothing. "I'm not that concerned about appearances. But I am a little worried about freezing my butt off when I head outside. Stay here. I'll grab something."

"Wait a minute. You're going out there?" It was a bizarre question, especially considering he was the sheriff and that the ranch was his property. It was reasonable that Lucas would be the one to check out things while Mark waited with her.

But to her heart, it didn't sound reasonable at all.

"Those kidnappers could be out there," she pointed out unnecessarily.

Lucas turned, stared at her. "Is this about what I think it's about?"

"Depends." She pulled the quilt around her. "If you

think it's about me having irrational feelings for a man I care about, then yes."

He seemed to ponder that a moment and then nodded. "I'm still going out there."

She hadn't thought for a second that her asinine rationalization would stop him. But she would try to figure out a way to make it as safe as she could possibly make it. Maybe they could request additional backup from Sheriff Knight so that Lucas wouldn't be alone during surveillance.

"I'll be right back," he told her. Still crouching, he made his way out of the room and into the hall.

Kylie sat there on the floor, snuggled in the warm blanket, and listened. She could hear Lucas moving around in his room. She could hear the winter wind push against the windows.

And she heard the crunching sound again.

Lucas must have heard it as well, because he barreled back down the hall and into the guest room. While he kept a firm grip on his Glock, he pulled on a pair of jeans, a sweatshirt and his boots.

The sound came again.

Lucas and she went stock-still. And Kylie tried to figure out what was going on. Not footsteps, exactly. Well, maybe that's what it was. As if the person or persons were dragging something. Worse, the last sound had been closer than the others. As if the sound makers were right outside the house.

Sweet merciful heaven.

If the kidnappers tried to get in, the alarms wouldn't be much of a deterrent. They could still bash through a door and start shooting. If that happened, Lucas and she would be forced to return fire. It could turn into a free-for-all with bullets flying.

And the baby could be hurt.

Or worse.

Her heart was pounding so hard that it surprised her that her ribs didn't crack, and the baby was doing flips or something, which didn't help with the pressure building inside her.

"Go ahead. Hum if it helps," Lucas suggested.

So, she did. Kylie tried out a few verses of "Silent Night," but then she stopped. Listened again. And realized what she wasn't hearing.

"Why didn't the dogs bark?" she asked.

"I don't know." Lucas answered quickly enough and without any surprise, making her realize he'd already considered that. And it was troubling him.

Because the Dobermans barked at strangers. Heck, they barked at friends. They just plain barked.

At everyone except Finn.

"Finn wouldn't do this," she whispered. And Kylie prayed that was true. Kidnapping, attempted murder and homicide were bad enough even when those heinous crimes hadn't been committed by a friend.

"He has no motive," Lucas added.

But did he?

Had something happened when he made those calls

for Cordelia? Had Finn gotten involved with something he shouldn't have?

Kylie shook her head. It just didn't mesh with the Finn she knew. As a teenager, he'd been a little wild. A lot weird. Somehow as much of a misfit as she'd been. But he wasn't a criminal.

"If someone gets in," Lucas instructed, "I don't want you to try to do anything heroic. I want you to hide."

"While you're getting shot at? Yeah. As if I could really do that. It's one thing to have you out doing a reconnaissance of the area, but it's totally different to stand by and watch someone shoot at you."

"I'm not giving you a choice, Kylie." He slid his left hand onto her stomach.

Her eyes narrowed. "That's dirty pool."

"I know. But it'll work. Because I know you care just as much about this baby as I do."

It was a powerful comment. One that she didn't want to admit was true. But it was. God help her, it was. Even though she'd tried to keep her feelings in check, she couldn't. She loved his baby with all her heart.

And then Lucas did something even more powerful. Even more amazing. He leaned over and brushed a kiss on her shocked, half-open mouth.

"Why do you do that?" she asked. Not as an accusation. Her tone was too dreamy.

But Lucas didn't get a chance to answer. There was

another noise. Something soft. It was merely the calm before the storm.

Seconds later, a bullet ripped through the window.

Chapter Fourteen

Lucas pushed Kylie down onto the floor. It wasn't a moment too soon. Broken glass burst across the room.

The bullet tore some of the wood from the window frame. The glass and the splinters created deadly fragments, one of which sliced across his arm.

His heart sprang to his throat. His muscles tightened. His body braced itself for a fight. A fight that some SOB had brought right to his home.

Lucas couldn't pinpoint the exact location of impact of the bullet, but it was somewhere in the general vicinity of the door—where he'd been standing just minutes earlier. For that matter, Kylie had been near there, as well. If they hadn't taken precautions, they could have been killed. And Lucas realized this wasn't over. The person firing those shots likely wouldn't stop until they were dead, so maybe all the precautions in the world wouldn't help them.

Adjusting his weapon, Lucas moved Kylie away from the wall, in case the shooter was using armor-piercing artillery that would go through layers of wood, insulation and dry wall.

"You're bleeding," she whispered.

Lucas glanced at the cut on his left forearm, specifically at the splatters of blood around it and dismissed it. "It's nothing."

He pushed her into the closet and crawled toward to the window so he could try to return fire.

The shooter beat him to it.

There was another shot. It slammed through what was left of the glass and created a deafening blast that filled the room. This time, he saw the point of impact. The bullet smashed into the wall near the door and sent bits of chalky material flying through the air.

Lucas felt the sting of the debris on his face. He felt the fear. It clawed its way through him, setting off a dozen nightmarish memories. Of his wife's shooting. A woman he hadn't been able to save.

Hell.

This had to stop. He couldn't risk a bullet ricocheting off something and hitting Kylie. Or himself. Because if anything happened to him, then that would likely leave Kylie and the baby at the mercy of people who probably hadn't come here to show much mercy.

Lucas made it to the window, took a quick look. Saw the barn. The yard.

But no shooter.

If it was only one shooter. There could be two or more. And there were a lot of places for gunmen to hide.

Assessing those places one at a time, he glanced out the window for fractions of seconds before pulling back. Each time he was able to exclude a particular hiding place.

Until he got to the storage shed positioned only about ten yards or so from the guest room window.

The moonlight helped with the open areas, but it also cast shadows around that storage shed. If he were planning on an ambush, that would be his choice for a hiding place. Plenty of cover. Proximity to the house. Easy access into the pasture and the woods in case an escape route was needed.

"Lucas, stay down!" Kylie ordered.

"I think I know where the shooter is."

"That won't help if you get your head blown off. Let's wait him out."

Lucas considered that and thought of his deputy, who was probably still miles out. In one way, not good, because he could certainly use the backup, but it also meant Mark Jensen wouldn't be driving straight into the line of fire.

"Call Mark," he instructed Kylie, tossing her the phone. "Tell him what's going on. He's not to approach the house. It's too dangerous."

Lucas stayed near the window, still crouching and peering out, and he stayed in a position to fire. Which he would certainly do once he verified the location of the shooter. No use wasting ammunition or giving away his own position to whoever was out there.

Behind him, he heard Kylie make the call. Listened to her voice as she briefed Mark. She sounded calm. Lucas knew she wasn't. She was terrified, not just for herself but for the baby. Somehow, some way, he had to get her out of this.

Why hadn't the dogs barked?

That question kept repeating in his head, but Lucas figured he wouldn't have an answer until he could get outside and take a look around. That wasn't going to happen with a shooter out there. He couldn't risk leaving Kylie alone, and Mark wouldn't proceed onto the property until he'd gotten some kind of okay from Kylie or him.

The silence returned. Lucas hated it. Because the gunman could still be moving closer to the house to get off a more accurate shot.

Lucas levered himself slightly and aimed. Rather than risk having the gunman getting an even better position, Lucas squeezed the trigger of his Glock. There was the lightning-fast recoil. A familiar feeling that he had no trouble controlling. His bullet slammed into the metal storage shed.

And then all hell broke loose.

Bullets came at the house.

Lots of them.

Not a single shot, but a barrage of deadly gunfire all pointed right at the window. However, those latest shots gave him his answer—there were two gunmen. At least. Because he could distinguish the sounds of at least

two different weapons. So now he had to wonder—
were they outnumbered? Outgunned? And if so, by how
much?

Lucas quickly checked on Kylie. She was still on the
floor of the closet, her arms covering her head, her gun
gripped in her hands. She wasn't out of danger, not by
a long shot, but at least she wasn't trying to help him
return fire.

The hot metal from the bullets ripped through the
fabric of the curtain, and the winter wind caught the
shreds, snapping them like bullwhips. The temperature
in the room plunged so quickly that he could suddenly
see the foggy cloud left by his breath.

Each new round of gunfire gave him a punch of
adrenaline. His heart rate was off the scale. Still, he
didn't let his physical reactions cause him to lose focus.
He listened. Observed.

Processed.

The next shot came close. Too close. It smashed into
the window frame just to the left of Lucas's head.
However, the close call allowed him to pinpoint one of
the gunmen's locations. He or she was on the left side
of the storage shed.

Finally, there was a lull in the attack. For whatever
reason, the gunmen stopped. Maybe to reload. Maybe
to listen. Maybe to move closer. Lucas didn't care. This
was the opening he'd been waiting for.

Lucas fixed an image of the gunman's position in his
mind. He came up and returned fire. He focused his shot

directly at the left corner of the shed. To fire the second shot he moved just slightly to the right so it'd tear through the structure.

It did.

There were a few sparks, the sound of metal ripping through metal, which Lucas ignored. However, he didn't ignore the shadowy movement that he saw. He squeezed off another shot and kept on shooting. Aiming right for that sputter of movement.

Until he ran out of ammo.

"Here!" Kylie said. She scrambled out of the closet and slid her .357 toward him.

Lucas didn't waste any time. He tossed his Glock onto the bed, retrieved the .357 Magnum from the floor and came up ready to fire.

But there was nothing to fire at.

The shadow was gone.

Lucas held his position. Waited. And he listened. But the only sound he heard was the wind and Kylie humming.

"This isn't over," he mumbled. And then he cursed. Because he knew what this meant.

The moment his deputy arrived to stay with Kylie, nothing would stop him. Lucas was going after the person who'd just tried to kill them, and one way or another, there would be hell to pay.

"LUCAS HAS BEEN OUT THERE too long," Kylie complained to Deputy Mark Jensen. "And he's injured. He wouldn't even let me look at that cut on his arm. A scratch, he said. 'Nothing to be concerned about.'"

Mark made a sound. Not an agreement, by any means. Just a male grunt to indicate he'd heard her but that he intended to take no action.

Not that there was any action to take.

Before Lucas left to check the grounds, he'd ordered Mark not to let her out of his sight. For the past hour and a half, the young deputy had obeyed his boss's order to a tee. So, here Mark and she sat in the living room. No lights on. Only using minimal comments and annoying grunts to communicate with each other.

But the deputy kept his weapon ready and aimed.

Kylie understood the ready and aimed part. She, too, had her own gun gripped in her hands. And she was mentally ready if the kidnappers returned, made their way past Lucas and somehow got inside. It wasn't as if that didn't concern her. It did. But it concerned her more that Lucas was out there and they hadn't heard so much as a peep from him.

She shouldn't have let him go out there alone. After all, there were no guarantees that the shooters had left. They could be hiding, waiting....

And she was taking another trip down paranoia lane.

Of course, it was easy to do that, what with the fact that someone obviously wanted them dead.

Tiffany had been right. *They'll do whatever it takes to stop Kylie Monroe and Sheriff Creed.* In their case, *whatever it takes* had been a potentially fatal attack right in Lucas's own home. Kylie wondered how long it would be before either of them would feel safe again. Certainly not until the gunmen and their boss were caught.

She heard the key turn in the lock, and she jumped to her feet. So did Mark, and he caught her to stop her from running into the foyer. A moment later, they realized his vigilance wasn't necessary.

Lucas walked through the door.

"Are you all right?" she asked. Though it was a dumb question because he appeared to be fine. Other than signs of fatigue and ruddy cheeks from the cold weather, Lucas looked the same as when he'd walked out the door nearly an hour earlier.

"I'm okay," Lucas assured her.

He reset the alarm, holstered his Glock and walked into the living room. Kylie couldn't help herself. She went to him and pulled him into her arms. It was a brassy move because Mark was there and he probably would eventually let it slip that Lucas and she had been in too friendly an embrace. Lucas obviously didn't care about the potential gossip because he returned the hug.

"The dogs are questionable," Lucas told her, saying it loud enough so that his deputy could hear. "It appears someone drugged them. I called Finn. He's on his way over to pick them up so he can take them to the vet."

"Drugged?" Kylie repeated. She pulled back so she could face him and examine his eyes to see what he was thinking. "So the gunmen had come prepared." It also meant that Finn wasn't behind any of this. He couldn't have risked drugging his beloved pets.

Well, he wouldn't have risked it unless he knew there was no chance that they'd actually be harmed. But she already had enough to concern her without dwelling on such an outside possibility.

"I'll make sure all the doors and windows are locked," Mark volunteered.

Kylie waited until the deputy was out of earshot before she continued. She also took off Lucas's buckskin jacket so she could check that cut on his arm.

"Finn was at his house when you called him?" she whispered.

The muscles in Lucas's jaw tightened. "He said he was."

"Any doubts?"

"His calls are automatically forwarded to his cell phone."

Her stomach sank to her knees. "Oh."

"Yes, *oh*."

So their old friend wasn't totally in the clear after all. Too bad. It would help if she could be sure that someone other than fellow law enforcement officers were on their side.

Kylie draped his coat over the back of the chair and rolled up his shirt sleeve. "Could someone like Cordelia have gotten close enough to drug the dogs?"

"Maybe. I found them in the pasture. Both had been shot with tranquilizer darts."

In other words, the perpetrator wouldn't have had to get that close to the dogs. That meant almost anyone could have done it. Well, anyone with a grudge against them, and that obviously included Cordelia.

Kylie frowned when she made her way to Lucas's injured forearm. Not a precise cut but an angry gash nearly two inches long. "Come with me to the bathroom so I can clean that."

He looked at her. "You know how to treat wounds?"

"No. Actually, I don't, but I figure I can find some antiseptic or something to stop it from getting infected. I don't suppose you'd consider seeing a doctor?"

"Nope."

But he did go with her down the hall after he slipped his arm around her waist. Not a totally intimate, cozy gesture on his part. She suspected that he was eager to get her away from any of the windows.

"I talked to Sergeant O'Malley at SAPD," Lucas explained. "She might be able to arrange for us to stay at a safe house."

"How safe is safe?" Kylie questioned. She located a bottle of hydrogen peroxide and bandages and got to work.

"Safer than here," he qualified. "In the meantime, Sheriff Knight is sending over one of his deputies to do horseback patrol. The county CSI guys are on the way, as well. They'll be combing the grounds for anything forensic they can use to identify the gunmen."

She dabbed on some of the hydrogen peroxide and blew on it so it wouldn't sting. "You've been busy."

"Yes. After the fact."

Mercy, he sounded bone-tired and weary. "Lucas, you didn't do anything wrong."

He shook his head. "I didn't do anything right, either."

That brought her nursing duties to a halt so she could stare at him. "Excuse me? We're alive. So is the baby. That's a lot of *right* as far as I'm concerned."

He didn't get a chance to dispute that because Mark Jensen appeared in the doorway of the bathroom.

"Anything else you want me to do?" Mark asked.

"No." Lucas took the bandage from her, slapped it on his arm and shoved his shirtsleeve back in place. "I have to board up that window the gunmen shot out."

"I'll do it," Mark volunteered.

"Thanks. There's some plywood and a toolbox in the barn."

Mark stepped away, but then he turned back toward them. "Any chance the dogs will wake up anytime soon? Those Dobermans don't like me much."

"They're snoozing like babies. And Finn should be here any minute to get them." Lucas snared her gaze after Mark left. "Finn won't be coming in. I told him you were shaken up, that you needed to get some rest."

She nodded. Kylie didn't mind being used as an excuse, mainly because she really didn't want to face their old friend, who might not have such friendly intentions toward them.

"So we're staying here tonight?" she asked.

"The safe house won't be ready for at least twenty-four hours, but don't worry. Knight's deputy will be outside on the grounds. So will the crime scene guys. And as a precaution, I want you to stay in my room."

That got her attention. "With you?"

"With me." It had a *duh* ring to it. "You have a problem with that?"

"No."

"You're sure?" he questioned.

"Of course not. It's just that people will know. They'll talk."

"Then let them talk." He gave an exhausted-sounding huff and led her in the direction of his bedroom. "I want you to get some sleep."

"But the crime scene guys—"

"I told them that we'd lock down for the night so they could secure the perimeter of the house for their investigation. I doubt the gunmen will want to make a return visit with all the activity going on."

True. In fact, for tonight anyway, the ranch was probably the safest place for them. Unfortunately, that didn't make her feel as certain as it should have. Absolute security probably wasn't in the cards until the people responsible were behind bars.

He opened the door to his bedroom. It was the first time she'd seen it. Like the rest of the house, it was dark. But even if she hadn't known it was Lucas's room, she would have been able to tell.

It smelled like him.

Something warm, musky and masculine. Something that immediately made her feel as if this was the place she wanted to be. Ironic, what with all the bullets that'd come their way tonight.

The cover was already drawn back, but he urged her into bed, and pulled the sheet and quilt over her. The bedding smelled like him, as well.

"While I had Sgt. O'Malley on the phone," he told her, "she said tomorrow afternoon they're going to bring in both Kendrick Windham and Isaac Dupont for questioning."

Finally! "I want to be there. I want to see the looks on their weaselly little faces when the cops ask them about Tiffany Smith and about what happened here tonight."

"Figured that. I want to be there, as well. But I don't want to take any unnecessary risks."

Kylie nodded. "There are risks whether we take them or not, Lucas. Heck, just breathing is a risk with those kidnappers, aka gunmen, on the loose."

"I know. That's why I asked if we could be present during questioning. Not in the room. But we'll be able to observe through the two-way mirror."

Well, it wasn't as good as being able to question them herself, but it would have to do. Besides, this was their best shot at getting some answers.

It had to work, because the alternative was unthinkable.

They couldn't continue to live like this. All the stress

wasn't good for the baby. Nor was it good for Lucas or her. Both of them needed to get on with their lives.

"What about you?" she asked. "Aren't you going to try to get some rest?"

"I'm resting." He climbed onto the bed with her. Right next to her. But he stayed on top of the covers. Boots and all. That *all* included his shoulder holster, weapon and even extra magazines of ammunition.

"You aren't going to get much sleep, are you?" she asked.

"No. But it's my guess you won't either."

He was right. Sleep, especially a peaceful sleep, wasn't a possibility. Not with the gunmen and kidnappers still at large. So Kylie snuggled closer to Lucas and let the silence settle in around them.

Chapter Fifteen

The cold spell had finally run its course. For the first time in days, Lucas didn't feel the need to bundle up when he opened the truck door so he could step out into the afternoon winter air.

Kylie opened her door as well.

But Lucas didn't let her get far.

While still within the meager protection of the truck, he took her arm before she could make her way into the SAPD headquarters building. "Here are the rules. You don't leave my side, and you don't take any chances."

She paused, pursed her lips. "Why do you get to make the rules?"

Lucas couldn't think of good reason, so he gave her the only one that came to mind. "Because I'm a cop and because I'm bigger than you."

She made a sound of amusement. "Size matters?" she questioned.

"You bet it does." In this case, anyway. If it came

down to it, his body would make a great human shield to protect her.

"Hardly seems fair," Kylie pointed out.

"Yeah." Because the amusement in her tone was forced and meant to soothe him, Lucas went for some levity that would hopefully soothe her. "And I know it contradicts what men have been saying for years. Still, this is a rare instance. But it should help that I have your best interest at heart."

Lucas didn't make that last comment lightly, either. It was true in every sense of the word. Gone were the hurt and resentment caused by Marissa's death. Yes, there was still grief. Always would be. But the anger was no longer there.

It was a relief to be rid of it.

He'd yet to tell Kylie that he'd forgiven her, but somewhere amid all those shots being fired at them, he realized he had done exactly that. There was nothing like a near-death experience to get a little perspective and camaraderie.

Unfortunately, near-death experiences could also get them killed.

He had to make sure the kidnappers/gunmen didn't get another opportunity to attempt that.

Lucas got out of the truck and hurried to the passenger's side. He pulled Kylie into the crook of his arm, sheltering her, while he kept his shoulder holster and weapon discreetly accessible. He got them moving quickly into the building. They'd barely stepped to the entry when they came face-to-face with Kendrick Windham.

No gym clothes today. He looked very much the part of the successful surrogacy clinic director. A polished tobacco-colored business suit. Pricey shoes. Equally pricey haircut. His expression was different, as well, in that it wasn't as disinterested and detached as it had been when Lucas had seen him at the hospital. Still, Windham might well have been nicknamed the iceman at the moment.

"Are you two the reason I was summoned here?" Windham immediately asked.

So he'd put two and two together. It was exactly what Lucas had expected him to do. Yet another reason for precautions. "*You're* the reason you're here," Lucas countered.

"Am I supposed to know what that means?"

Since Windham was looking directly at Kylie, or rather staring at her, she was the one who responded. "Tiffany Smith is dead. Someone tried to kill us. The police want answers, and they're looking to get those answers from you. Hence, the summons."

"Then both you and the police are going to be disappointed. But then you obviously must know that, or you wouldn't have requested Isaac Dupont to come here this afternoon, as well. Hedging your bets, I assume. If you can't get me to confess, you'll try to browbeat him." He turned that acid gaze on Lucas and hissed out a breath. "I didn't mind your courtesy call to tell me about Tiffany being hospitalized, but I won't tolerate you trying to frame me for crimes I didn't commit."

Lucas shrugged, trying to appear calm. But there was no way he could remain calm with this man so close to Kylie. It didn't matter that there were two armed officers less than ten feet away. It also didn't matter that they were inside a building crammed full of surveillance cameras and cops who could respond at the first sign of trouble. Lucas still felt as if Kylie were being threatened.

"If you didn't do anything wrong," Lucas informed Windham, "then you don't have anything to worry about."

"You're right, of course. But you and Ms. Monroe apparently do have something to worry about. Oh, and let's not forget Isaac Dupont. I'm sure he has a ton of worries right now, what with the allegations of his wrongdoing. Those allegations could destroy his career, and he won't care for that," he said, his tone placating. Definitely not a good sign. "I, too, have friends in law enforcement."

"And these friends told you about Dupont being called in for an interview?" Lucas asked.

"That, and I also heard about the shooting last night at your place."

Lucas didn't like the sound of that, or the implications. If Windham did have connections in SAPD, then he could possibly learn the location of the safe house that the San Antonio police were arranging. That would mean Windham or God knew who else would know where they'd be.

Sitting ducks was the term that came to mind.

When the interviews were finished, he'd have to come up with other arrangements to keep Kylie safe.

Since this conversation had already taken a bad turn, Lucas decided it was time to go for Windham's jugular. "Did you hire the people who fired those shots at us last night?"

Windham laughed. The sound was smoky and thick. Not placating. He'd moved on to blatant mockery. "I'm not in the habit of hiring hit men."

"That wasn't what I asked," Lucas pointed out.

"I know." Windham coupled that remark with one last icy glance, and turned, calmly put his trim leather briefcase on the conveyor belt and stepped through the metal detector. He breezed right through and disappeared down one of the corridors, apparently headed for the interview room.

Because Lucas was armed, it took Kylie and him longer to get through security. Then they had to wait for Sgt. Katelyn O'Malley to come down to the lobby so she could escort them to the observation area.

"We have a glitch," Sgt. O'Malley immediately informed them. The tall, athletic-looking redhead motioned for them to follow her.

"Does it have anything to do with the info leaked to Windham?" Lucas wanted to know.

That caused the sergeant to slow a bit so she could make eye contact. "What kind of info?"

"He knew about the shooting at my ranch."

"Ah, that. Windham could have gotten it from a variety of sources. Maybe even here," she admitted. Huffing, she plowed her fingers through the side of her hair and briefly tipped her eyes to the ceiling. "People talk, and they aren't always careful about anyone who might be listening."

Well, that did it. The safe house was definitely out.

"The glitch I was referring to is Isaac Dupont," O'Malley continued. "He showed up about a half hour ago and demanded we start the interview earlier than we'd planned. Said he has an appointment that he can't reschedule."

Yet more bad news. Lucas hoped this wasn't a trend. There were already enough strikes against them without adding more.

"So we missed the interview?" Kylie asked.

"Just about." Sgt. O'Malley checked her watch. "I'm sure the detective will be wrapping things up soon. Dupont isn't exactly the poster child for patience. I suspect he'll be whining to get out of there as quickly as possible. But we're taping the session so you'll be able to see it."

Lucas knew it wasn't as good as witnessing the actual session, but it would have to do.

Sgt. O'Malley glanced over her shoulder at them again. "Oh, and get this. Dupont didn't arrive alone. He lawyered up."

"A lawyer who lawyers up," Lucas mumbled. Maybe it was a weird kind of show of power or just a simple attempt to cover his butt. Either way, it meant Dupont likely wasn't going to say anything of any value.

Hell.

Lucas really needed a break soon. Kylie's and their child's safety depended on it.

He stopped when he realized the thought that had just passed through his head.

Their child.

Not *his*.

Theirs.

When the devil had that happened?

Was the shooting and the camaraderie responsible for that, as well? Of course, it could have been that whole making-out session against the door. That certainly had a way of breaking down old issues. He couldn't pinpoint the timing, but he couldn't deny what he felt.

"Are you okay?" he heard Kylie ask.

Lucas pulled himself away from his musings to realize that both women had stopped, as well, and they were staring at him.

"I'm fine," he insisted.

And he started walking again so that neither Sgt. O'Malley nor Kylie would ask any more questions. Instead, he needed to focus on the remaining interview with Isaac Dupont and then with Kendrick Windham. After all, Kylie and he were literally under the same roof as two potential killers. That had to take priority over any turmoil he was feeling about his relationship, or lack thereof, with Kylie.

The sergeant led them into the observation room,

and on the other side of the two-way mirror, Lucas saw Isaac Dupont, another guy in a navy suit who had lawyer written all over him and the officer who was doing the interview. Dupont was in the middle of what appeared to be an explanation as to his whereabouts the prior evening. Specifically, the time of the shooting at the ranch.

"My alibi will check out," Dupont declared. He said it with too much confidence for Lucas to believe it was anything other than the truth. No surprise there. If Dupont had indeed hired the gunmen, then he would have insured he had an airtight alibi so that no one could trace the crime to him.

"Talk to me about Tiffany Smith," the detective insisted.

Dupont and his lawyer exchanged glances, and it was his attorney who answered. "My client has no personal or professional connection to Ms. Smith."

"Sheesh. It took a sidebar with his lawyer to come up with that puny answer?" Kylie mumbled.

Lucas made a sound of agreement. "He didn't exclude an *illegal* connection with Tiffany, though." And that was the only one that mattered. Something that would connect Dupont to the illegal surrogacy activity and therefore to Kylie's article and the attempts on their lives.

But Dupont obviously wasn't just going to hand them that information.

Lucas watched as the detective wrapped up the interview. Dupont and his lawyer stood. They even exchanged friendly handshakes with the detective, and Dupont promised if he thought of any additional information to help the police, then he would call them right away.

Hell would freeze over first.

"You're just going to let him go?" Kylie asked Sgt. O'Malley. Because it was asked out of sheer frustration, she waved off her own question. Since Kylie was a former cop, she knew SAPD had no legal reason to hold either Dupont or even Windham. These interviews were basically fishing expeditions, and so far they hadn't caught anything. Lucas didn't think Windham would slip up either.

Kylie reached for the doorknob, but Lucas stopped her. "Going somewhere?" he asked.

"I want to talk to Dupont."

That's exactly what he thought she had in mind, and it was exactly what wasn't going to happen. "Remember our size and rules discussion?"

Her hands went on her hips. "You think Dupont will pull out a gun and try to kill me here? I wish. If he did something totally brainless like that, then Sgt. O'Malley could arrest him, and this would all be over."

Kylie didn't wait for him to agree. Ignoring the rules and Lucas's glare—which he knew was a top-notch expression—she opened the door and stepped into the hall. Sgt. O'Malley and Lucas were right behind her. The only person missing was Dupont. He was still in the interview room.

"As you requested, we're also looking into the financials on your former sister-in-law, Cordelia Landrum," Sgt. O'Malley told Lucas.

"And?" He was very much interested in what the sergeant had to say, but he also started jockeying for position with Kylie. So that he was between her and the interview room.

"I haven't found anything on Ms. Landrum so far," Sgt. O'Malley explained. "But she has a lot of money and money trails to sort through, including an offshore account. Even a warrant won't get me into that. Don't worry, though. I'll keep at it, and something might turn up."

So Cordelia wasn't in the clear. Though she wouldn't have gotten her hands dirty with the actual kidnapping and shooting, she could have hired someone to do those things.

Just like Dupont.

Just like Windham.

Lucas left Finn's name off that list because, thankfully, he hadn't been able to come up with a solid motive. So far, the only thing he could accuse Finn of was being badgered into helping Cordelia find out about the surrogacy. Hardly a crime. Well, maybe Finn could be disciplined for breaching a patient's confidentiality, but he likely wasn't involved in a felony.

The door of the interview room opened, and Lucas did a little sidestepping to stop Kylie from violating Dupont's personal space. Judging from the man's unpleasant expression, it wouldn't be a good time to provoke him.

"Sheriff Creed," Dupont said, smiling a smile that no one on Earth would have mistaken as genuine. "And your trusty sidekick, Kylie Monroe. Always turning up at the oddest places, aren't you?"

"I'm a cop. This is cop headquarters," Lucas pointed out. "This isn't that odd of a place for me to be. Besides, I heard you were in the building." Lucas intentionally used the same cocky phrasing Dupont had when he had made his appearance at the hospital.

"And you just couldn't wait to see me." Dupont's gaze slipped past Lucas and went to Kylie. "How is the little mom-to-be?"

"Peachy," Kylie let him know in her best sarcastic tone. "Well, except for someone shooting at us. You wouldn't know anything about that, would you?" Oh, butter wouldn't melt in that mouth.

However, Kylie's cool talking had no effect on Dupont. "No. Why don't you ask Kendrick Windham?"

"Because he would only point the finger at you."

"Yes." Now, there was a genuine smile. A smug one. "The finger-pointing creates reasonable doubt, doesn't it? A sort of he said, he said."

"Reasonable doubt can be eliminated with a little proof." Lucas put his hand on Kylie's arm to get them moving. He didn't want her near Dupont any longer.

Fortunately, Kylie cooperated, and they turned to

follow Sgt. O'Malley back into the observation room so they'd be in place for Windham's interview.

"What—no Wild West threats about getting me no matter what it takes?" Dupont called out. "Personally, I think both of you are a threat of the worst kind."

That stopped Lucas. Kylie stopped, as well. But neither of them turned back to face Dupont.

"I don't like people who cause for trouble for me," Isaac Dupont warned. "My advice? Think about that when you try to sleep tonight."

Chapter Sixteen

Kylie took her prenatal vitamin and washed it down with a few gulps of milk. With that daily task finished, she sat on the sofa and listened to Lucas do one of the things he did best—be a cop.

Earlier, after they'd left SAPD headquarters, he'd called and arranged for a private security guard and a neighboring deputy sheriff to patrol the ranch. Now he was in contact with both of them and was giving instructions as to where they should set up security and surveillance.

Along with Sheriff Knight's deputy, that would give them three extra pairs of hands in case the gunmen decided to make a return visit. The extra hands were necessary because despite other phone calls, it appeared Lucas wasn't having much luck securing them a safe house.

That probably meant staying at the ranch again.

It was going to be a *long* night.

Kylie tried not to let the concern register on her face or in her body language. Hard to suppress something like that, though, especially since they still had a boarded-up window from the previous night's attack.

The entire house was dark; the only light came from the moon, and those meager rays filtered in through the edges of the plantation blinds and curtains, which were all shut tight, as well. Neither Lucas nor she had gone near a window. And the alarms were set. All the doors were double-locked.

They hadn't stopped there. Both of them had their shoulder holsters, guns and extra magazines of ammunition lying on the coffee table just inches away. Wherever they went tonight, the guns and ammo would go with them.

Lucas ended his call and sank down on the sofa next to her. "I haven't given up. I'm still trying to arrange for a place for us to stay."

"And let me guess—you're not going through SAPD to do that?" Kylie asked.

"Not after hearing Kendrick Windham brag about the *friends* he has in law enforcement."

Yes, that had unnerved her, too. Of course, Windham hadn't brought up that point during the interview with the SAPD detective. Kylie had listened for any nuance of a threat or any shred of useful information.

Nothing.

Windham had been cordial. Polite, even. Definitely not menacing. But the damage had already been done. Well, if there could be any more damage to her peace of mind. She wasn't sure she had any peace of mind left.

"I don't want us to arrive at a safe house only to discover that it's a trap," Lucas added. "I considered a hotel."

Kylie was already shaking her head before he had finished. "Too hard to secure. Plus, we could endanger civilians if the shooter opened fire. And I have no doubt that he or she is gutsy enough to open fire regardless of the collateral damage it'd cause."

He nodded. "There's the jail," he pointed out.

The drawback was that it was literally in the center of Fall Creek, surrounded by shops, businesses and homes. "It wouldn't be any easier to secure than the ranch. Not unless you're willing to deputize the entire town."

"That's a scary thought. There are some people you just don't want to have in control of a deadly weapon."

Yes. At least a dozen came to mind.

Finn included.

Lucas blew out a weary breath. "We could just leave, drive to the airport in San Antonio or Houston and get on the first plane that's headed out of the state."

She'd thought of that, too. "What if the person responsible for this has us followed? Then, we're in Bermuda or wherever, and we have no backup. Plus, we wouldn't even be able to carry our guns on the plane. When we landed, we'd be practically defenseless." She paused, noted the additional frustration that her answer caused Lucas. "Staying here isn't exactly my first choice, either, but I think we need to stay put until we're certain we have something safer."

He met her gaze. "You're being awfully rational about this."

She laughed. "Then appearances can indeed be deceiving. Because beneath all this milk sipping and prenatal vitamin popping, I'm shaken to the core."

She'd tried to say it lightly enough, so that it didn't put more pressure on him, but he obviously saw through the filmsy pretense. He slid his hand over hers, linking their fingers together.

"I'm just worried this could go on for weeks," she admitted.

Or months.

Or forever.

Kylie didn't dare voice that. She was having a hard enough time trying to get past the next five minutes. She wasn't ready to deal with forever yet.

"I think it'll all come to a head soon." Lucas rotated his shoulder, testing it, and she realized he was actually testing the wound on his arm. Judging from the slight wince he made, it still hurt. "Neither Dupont or Windham were pleased about being called in for interviews. Plus, Sgt. O'Malley is digging into Cordelia's financials."

"Cordelia won't be happy about that. She'll have her lawyers suing everyone in sight."

Of course, a lawsuit seemed positively benign compared to everything else going on.

Kylie finished her milk, set the glass on the coffee table and freed herself from Lucas's grip so her hands would be free to unbutton the cuff on his dark blue shirt.

He'd changed clothes since they'd returned from San Antonio, and when she couldn't shove up the sleeve of this particular shirt far enough, she went after the front buttons.

He looked at her and even in the moonlight, she could see the questioning expression. "It's Florence Nightingale time?"

She nodded. "I'm going to check that wound."

"You mean that scratch," he immediately corrected.

"Men always say that. You could be gushing arterial spray, and it'd still be a scratch." The joke didn't settle well in her stomach. Neither did the sight of the *scratch* when she eased the shirt off his shoulder and gently peeled back the bandage. It was a brutal reminder of how close he'd come to being killed.

"You're frowning," Lucas pointed out.

She forced the frown away. Lucas had too much to deal with without her adding to his troubles. "I just wanted an excuse to get your clothes off."

"You don't need an excuse for that."

She smiled and pressed the bandage back in place. "That sounded like a come-on."

He waited a moment, long enough for her to bring her gaze back to his. "What if it was?" he asked.

Oh.

Kylie's throat clamped shut. Not the best time for that to happen, because her silence seemed like an unspoken invitation.

Which it was.

Yes, she had a lot on her mind, what with the danger and the baby. But even with all of that, she hadn't been able to forget how it felt to have Lucas hold her and touch her. She especially hadn't been able to forget those kisses they'd shared. She'd relived them too many times to count. The taste of them. The taste of *him*. And she'd also daydreamed about getting close like that all over again.

What she felt for him was strong, overpowering and always there. Always. A slow, gnawing hunger. It made her feel alive. And terrified. Because there were times, like now, when she wondered how she could possibly live without him. Somewhere along the line, he'd become more important than anything to her.

Lucas didn't move, but the narrow space between them suddenly seemed to vanish. Her heart instantly went into overdrive. And where was the air? There definitely wasn't enough air in the living room. Maybe it was the lack of air that was suddenly making her light-headed. Or maybe it was his mouth. That sensuous made-for-kissing mouth that was so close she could taste it. Kylie was no longer sure what to hope for. One thing was certain—she wanted him.

And he obviously knew it.

He reached out and skimmed his fingers over her cheek. "You didn't answer. What if this is a come-on?"

She had to clear her throat so she could speak. "Then I'd have to question our sanity. Because we're not even sure if we're safe."

But Kylie barely heard her own argument.

Much less believed it.

Lucas obviously didn't believe it, either, because he pulled her into his lap. Kylie wasn't sure how he had accomplished that little feat. One moment, she was sitting on the sofa; the next moment, she was sitting on him.

All in all, not a bad place to sit.

She glanced down at their new position and gave it a nod of approval. Lucas gave it his own approval, as well. He moved against her. Softly. Body against body. Everything slowed. Like a lazy hot breeze. It swirled around her until all she could see and feel was Lucas.

He didn't kiss her. He just looked at her as if trying to decide if this was a good idea.

"You're cold?" he asked, his Texas drawl heightening the words.

The warm air from the ceiling vent was washing over her. And the room definitely wasn't cool. Maybe because of her penchant for not wearing shoes around the house, Lucas had really cranked up the heat.

In more ways than one.

Still, she was shivering. Actually honest-to-goodness shivering. And not because she was scared.

Okay, maybe she was a little scared.

She was scared that this was all just a very good dream, and that she would wake up and Lucas would be gone. Worse, he would still hate her. They'd still be at the hellish impasse where they'd been for three years.

But then, he slid his hand around the back of her neck. Eased her closer. His mouth came to hers. Barely a touch. Enough to reassure her that this was no dream but a flesh-and-blood man who wanted her.

"If you're going to say no, do it now," he warned.

"Why would I say no?" Her breasts brushed against his bare chest and sent her pulse right off the chart.

"Because you might be having doubts."

She dismissed that with a soft sound of denial. "Lucas, I feel a lot about you, *for* you, but I don't have those kinds of doubts."

He cupped her chin, slid his thumb over her bottom lip. There was gentleness in his touch. Almost reverence. *Almost.* But in his eyes, she could see the heat. The fire. The need. There was nothing reverent about that. Mercy, she wanted him.

And the next kiss proved it.

Roughly grabbing handfuls of his hair, she wrenched his mouth to hers. And she kissed him, all right. There were no more preliminaries, no long doubting looks, no soft caressing breaths, no gentleness. Just them. Two people kissing each other as if this would be the last kiss either of them would ever get to experience.

It worked. Both for her libido and for the rest of her. Lucas was melting the cold that for years she had allowed to seep into her blood and into her heart. He was somehow making her feel new again. Had anything felt this good, this all-consuming, this overwhelming?

This necessary?

No, she admitted honestly. Nothing.

And that's why Kylie knew it couldn't stop.

LUCAS HAD no intentions of stopping this time, but even if he'd had such intentions, they had gone south in a hurry. Frantically, he pulled at her stretchy top. Then he did a reversal.

And stopped.

His attention landed on her stomach, and his forehead bunched up. Along with that bunching came some doubts. Hell. His body didn't want any doubts. His body wanted to race full speed ahead and have wild, mindless sex. But that stomach was a cool reminder that his body wasn't calling the shots here.

"Pregnant women are allowed to have sex," Kylie assured him.

His forehead bunched up further. "I don't want to hurt you."

"Good." She exaggerated a breath of relief. "I'm not much into S and M anyway." She hooked her arm around his waist. "Let's just go with it, Lucas. Don't think about it."

He nodded. "Relying on extremely long-term memory here, sex isn't about thinking, anyway."

"I agree. Same long-term memory here. Same conclusion. Don't think. Just do it."

That was the invitation he'd been waiting for. And he didn't wait any longer. His mouth came to hers. Hot and hungry. His hands plowed into her hair, shoving it from her face so that nothing would be in the way.

Lucas hauled her against him, gently because of the pregnancy, but it got the job done. She fastened herself around him, her knees cradling his hips. On a strangled groan, her lips parted, and he took her mouth the way he wanted to take it.

He drew in a gulp of air through his mouth, inhaling in her taste and scent. It raced through him, stirring his blood and body in a way nothing else could. Man, he wanted her. Needed her. He had to have her now.

She moaned in response. It wasn't a soft moan, either. It was a lustful moan. A *thank-you* kind of sound that spilled from her mouth directly into his and became trapped within their kiss.

He devoured it.

Lucas went after her earlobes. First one and then the other, taking them in his mouth so his tongue could flirt with her satiny gold-star earrings. Against him, he felt her pulse race and her breath quicken.

Or was that his?

He couldn't tell any longer. They had pressed themselves together so tightly he couldn't tell where he stopped and she started.

Her hands quickly reminded him.

Yanking his shirt out of the waistband of the jeans, she delved underneath to his chest to explore. She sought out every muscle, every inch of skin, even the flat nipples buried in his chest hair, until the touching was apparently no longer enough. In a violent motion, she stripped the shirt over his head and sent it flying.

Stirring restlessly against him, Kylie kissed his neck, his collarbone, his shoulders. With her mouth, she retraced the path her hands had taken. Lucas grimaced and managed a strangled groan.

With a mutual effort, her garnet-red sweater came off. Her bra, a flimsy little swatch of ivory silk and lace, was only a few shades lighter than her pale skin. Her nipples were already tightened from arousal and peeked over the bra's lacy edges.

"Very nice," he said, though how he managed something like speech, he didn't know.

Slowly, keeping his eyes connected with hers, he lowered his mouth to one of those rosy nipples and nipped it with his teeth. Panting, from both anticipation and the fierce heat building inside her, Kylie grabbed him by the hair and pulled him to her, forcing him, until he took that nipple into his mouth. Leaving it shiny wet and pebbly hard, he gave the other one the same attention.

"I want more," Kylie insisted.

And she didn't wait. In a move that surprised him, she planted her feet on the sofa. Still straddling him, she rose to a near standing position so she could wiggle free of her loose black pants. Though she was obviously doing this to undress, Lucas took full advantage of it. He halted her in mid-descent by grasping her hips.

She looked down at him. Questioning. And trying to wriggle back onto his lap. Lucas stopped the wriggling.

He pressed his mouth to her stomach, circling her navel with his tongue.

"Yes." Kylie nodded.

He went slightly lower. To her panties. There was so little to them he wondered why she'd bothered at all. Definitely not the functional ones he'd gotten a glimpse of at the clinic. The same ivory color as the bra, the piece of silk had a lacy triangle that almost perfectly outlined the triangle of dark blond curls underneath.

"Yes. Yes," she repeated.

He loved hearing those yeses from her and decided to do something to make her keep saying it.

Lucas went even lower. Right to that narrowest point of the vee of lace. When his tongue touched her through that fragile barrier, her breath hitched, frozen in her throat. Her bottom lip trembled. She soundlessly pleaded for more.

He would definitely give her more.

"Please," she mumbled. "Yes."

It was the yes that flooded him with another jolt of fire. Lucas considered finishing her off right then, right there. He could have those panties off her in no time and put his mouth to good use. What would it be like to see her shatter? To taste her when he brought her to climax? He didn't think he could wait to find out.

He apparently thought about it too long, because Kylie dropped back down and went after his zipper. "I want you now," she announced. "Okay?"

As if he had plans to disagree.

"Lucas?" she whispered.

"Kylie," he answered.

"Watch," she demanded.

"I know who you are," he assured her. "I know *exactly* who you are. I'm glad it's you, Kylie. I want it to be you."

"Good," she mumbled, the one word sounding strangled.

With their gazes locked, his hands latched onto her hips, he entered her. Slowly. As gently and as carefully as their raging need would allow. Sliding hot and deep into her. Lucas stilled just for a second, to absorb and to understand. To savor.

A delicious little smile flickered on Kylie's mouth. And she said, "Yes."

There it was again. A jolt of fire caused by that one word. Lucas cursed, pressing his forehead against her cheek. This was madness and redemption all rolled into one. She was so wet, so snug, he figured this must be paradise. Of course, it might also be the most wicked sin hell had to offer, too. At the moment, he couldn't decide.

At the moment, he didn't think he knew his own name.

Guiding her hips with his hands, Lucas swept her against him, but Kylie soon moved into his rhythm until she took over the pace. She stunned him, pleasured him, until he thought he should beg for mercy. The only thing he knew for certain was he would want her again as soon as they finished. More frightening than that, he would want her tomorrow.

And the next day.

She moved against him until he felt her shiver. Until she was his pinpoint focus. Until all he could see was Kylie.

With her body closing around him, Lucas tossed back his head, the veins of his neck straining at the force of blood pumping through him.

And he went with her.

It was the only place he wanted to go.

Chapter Seventeen

"We may have discovered a cure for the common cold," Lucas commented between gulps of breath.

Kylie did some breath-gulping of her own. "Well, it was a cure for something, that's for sure." Kylie didn't mind that her lungs still felt starved for air. She didn't mind the giddy feeling, because every part of her hummed with contentment and pleasure.

"Regrets?" he asked.

"No way. You?"

In those few seconds that it took him to answer, Kylie felt as if she were waiting for the most important answer she'd ever hear. "My only regret is that I didn't add more foreplay." He slid his hand between their bodies and stroked her belly.

The relief made her smile. "There was nothing wrong with your foreplay. Or the sex." She kissed him, long and hard. "Or you."

Well, nothing wrong except she was falling in love

with him. There was no denying it. She was falling, and there was nothing she could do to stop it.

Should she tell him?

It was a risk either way. If she got up, stayed silent and let him think that this was just sex, she might not have another opportunity to tell him that, for her, they'd made love. And it'd changed everything.

The way she felt about him.

The way she felt about herself.

Yes, indeed. It had been a magic cure, and for the first time in three years she felt whole and healed.

And confused.

Because while making love with Lucas had been one of the most wonderful experiences of her life, she was already wondering where this would lead. And she had to admit to herself that it probably wouldn't lead where her heart was trying to take her.

Maybe this was it. All that would happen between them. A one-night stand, of sorts. Maybe in the morning, he'd realize what a mistake it had been and would tell her that he needed to back off. That old proverbial *I need space*. It wouldn't be a lie, either, since this would no doubt take him to a new level of guilt.

Lucas's cell phone rang. Both groaned when they had to break the intimate contact and pull away from each other. While Lucas located his phone in his jacket pocket, she located her pants, top and underwear. Best not to sit around naked in case one of the deputies or the guard was approaching the house.

"Sheriff Creed," she heard Lucas say to the caller. With the phone sandwiched between his shoulder and ear, he fixed his jeans and grabbed his shirt. "Finn, is that you?"

That got her attention. Not in a good way, either. And it frustrated her that it did. A call from Finn shouldn't have caused her adrenaline to kick in.

With her attention now glued to Lucas, Kylie stepped into her pants and pulled them on. She quickly did the same with her bra and top.

"The connection's bad," Lucas continued. "I didn't hear what you said." A pause. Then a few seconds later, he added. "And?"

Judging from his suddenly ramrod-straight posture and his tight jaw, whatever Finn was saying had captured Lucas's attention, as well.

"Okay. Of course, I'll tell her," Lucas said, and he pushed the End Call button. "Finn got back your test results from the blood he drew the night of the kidnapping attempt."

She certainly hadn't forgotten about that, or the drug that the kidnappers had used to try to sedate her. But with everything else going on, she'd put it in the back of her mind. It quickly moved to the forefront.

Kylie protectively slid her hand over her stomach. And waited.

"According to Finn, everything looks fine. The drug was chloroform, but it was in such small amounts that it won't harm the baby."

She released the breath that she didn't even know she'd been holding. It should have been wonderful news. A reason for celebration. But since the info had come Finn, it automatically came under suspicion.

"You think he'd lie about something like that?" Kylie asked.

Lucas shook his head, then shrugged. "I want the tests repeated as soon as we can safely get to your doctor in San Antonio."

Heaven knew when that might be.

However, Lucas was right. Despite all the danger, the baby was their number one priority, and somehow they'd have to find a way to redo that test.

Because Lucas looked weary and frustrated, Kylie went to him and took his hand. She placed it on her stomach and adjusted it so that his palm was just over the little bumps and kicks that the baby was making.

"He or she is healthy," Kylie promised, though both knew it was a promise she had no control over. "By Father's Day, you'll be holding your child in your arms, and everything that's happening now will be just unpleasant memories."

He stared at her a moment as if considering that. "You'll be leaving when the baby's born."

It wasn't a question. More like a confirmation. It seemed as if he were waiting for her to deny it. But she couldn't. Even after making love to him only minutes earlier, she didn't have a clue if they had a future. He certainly hadn't asked her to be in his future.

Or the baby's.

Kylie opened her mouth—to say what exactly, she didn't know. Lucas opened his mouth, as well. Closed it. She closed hers too. And they stood there staring at each other. Apparently waiting for the other to make the first move.

The noise interrupted them both.

There was loud crash. Not exactly a foreign sound, either. It was glass shattering followed by something metallic landing on the floor. The sound had come from the kitchen.

God, was someone breaking into the house? And if so, where the devil were the deputies and the guard? No one should have gotten close enough to break in.

She grabbed her gun and turned to rush toward that noise, but Lucas caught her arm to stop her. He snatched up his own shoulder holster and weapon and practically pushed her back onto the sofa.

"Stay down," he warned.

Kylie did. Only because she didn't want to break his suddenly intense concentration. But she strapped on her shoulder holster, as he did, and drew her weapon so she'd be ready to react.

Lucas inched toward the sound, using the furniture and the wall as cover. Kylie watched as he peered around the edge of the arched entryway that led into the kitchen.

He cursed.

Then he put his hand to his mouth and coughed.

She started to ask what was wrong, but the question wasn't necessary. Kylie saw the wispy smoke and caught the scent of something pungent that immediately caused her to cough.

"It's tear gas!" Lucas shouted.

His cough-punctuated shout was muted somewhat by yet more breaking glass. Also in the kitchen. The sound was followed by another metal object landing on the clay-tiled floor. Probably another canister of tear gas because the yellow smoke seemed to double in volume.

And intensity.

Sweet heaven. The kidnappers had obviously returned, and they were trying to flush them out of the house.

She clamped her hand over her mouth, but that didn't stop the fumes from making their way into her eyes, nose and throat. Mercy, she couldn't breathe. Could barely see. And her lungs burned.

Somehow Lucas made it to her, though he was coughing, as well. He grabbed her arm and got them moving down the hall, away from the fumes. But the fumes seemed to be right on their heels, swallowing them up. Her first instinct was to head outside, to the fresh air, but that's was exactly what the kidnappers wanted them to do. Once outside, Lucas and she would likely be ambushed. Of course, staying inside didn't appeal too much, either.

She needed air, and she needed it now.

Lucas shoved open the door to the nursery, and they

hurried inside. Kylie gulped in a much needed breath and detected only a trace of the tear gas in the room. But it wouldn't be long before it seeped into every part of the house. Worse, there was another shattering of glass.

Another canister landed inside.

She hadn't needed that third canister to know they were in trouble, but it seemed to be the punctuation mark that sent her heart pounding.

The pounding only got worse when she detected another scent.

Smoke.

Real smoke.

Not from a tear gas canister, either.

Lucas whipped around to face her, and in the same motion, he lifted his head and sniffed. "Hell," he grumbled. "The house is on fire. Let's move."

At first, Kylie thought that Lucas might have planned for them to escape through the window, but he elbowed the door closed, locking them in. Then he grabbed the crib box and shoved it against the bottom of the door to create a barricade from the smoke and tear gas. A temporary barricade, because fire could easily eat through that.

Lucas reached for the pull cord that drew down the wooden attic flap. He unfolded the stairs and stepped on the first rung.

"Stay right behind me," Lucas insisted. "I need to make sure it's safe up here."

She glanced over her shoulders and saw that tear gas had started to ooze in around the doorframe.

Lucas paused at the top step, looked around and then motioned for her to join him. Kylie didn't waste any time because each passing second brought in more of the fumes and smoke. She'd dealt with tear gas during her training at the police academy, but she had no idea if this would harm the baby. And here she'd just received assurance from Finn that all was well as to the effects of the chloroform. That should have been reason for celebration. Or at least relief. Instead, she'd bypassed the relief stage and had been launched into a terrifying ordeal that she might not survive.

Kylie tried not to let the fear take hold of her. She didn't want to die. Not here. Not like this with her unborn child still inside her. But the adrenaline was screaming for her to run. To do something—anything— to escape. It was a powerful, overwhelming sensation.

Fight or flight.

Even if either option could get her killed.

"We're going to get out of this," she heard Lucas say. Maybe he'd sensed her thoughts. Or maybe she looked terrified. The humming was a dead giveaway, too. Kylie didn't care what'd prompted his response. She held on to it like a lifeline and followed Lucas into the attic.

The floorboards creaked beneath them as they meandered their way through the cluttered space. Cardboard boxes and trunks were crammed against the walls, but there was ample space for them to walk toward the attic vent at the far end.

Kylie forced herself to concentrate on her breathing.

It wouldn't be a good time to hyperventilate. Besides, things were already in motion. If the kidnappers were out there waiting for them, there would be a shootout. She didn't want to speculate about who would win.

They had to win.

Their baby's life was at stake.

Lucas reached the far end of the attic first. There wasn't a window there, but a large porthole of sorts with vented slats. He yanked out those slats, leaving them a venue to fire at attackers or, if that failed, a means of escape.

Well, maybe.

Kylie peered out into the moonlit yard. She didn't see any gunmen or kidnappers. Nor any sign of the deputies or guard. There were just ghostly wisps of smoke and a whole lot of open space between them and the pasture. Still, if they could get out of the house and to the pasture, then they could use the surrounding woods as cover.

Lucas continued to watch the yard. And cursed. Which probably meant he didn't see their attackers, either. "I need to climb out on the roof."

Kylie shook her head, but the nonverbal disapproval was useless. Because she knew Lucas was going to go out there anyway.

He *had* to.

There was no other choice.

The house was on fire; if they stayed put, they'd be

burned alive. And they couldn't just go barreling out into the yard, either or they'd be gunned down.

Lucas grabbed a portable steel chain escape ladder that was attached to the wall and unrolled it. He shoved it onto the roof and brushed a kiss on her cheek. "Stay put until I give the okay."

He didn't wait for her to agree. Lucas used one of the nearby boxes for leverage so he could hoist himself through the porthole. He landed on his belly and immediately repositioned his gun so he'd be ready to fire.

Kylie didn't take her attention off him, but she was aware that smoke was beginning to fill the attic. She didn't think it was her imagination that it was getting hotter, too. She could hear the flames devouring the house.

So that she'd be able to breathe, she moved closer to the porthole. Closer to the fresh air. And she aimed her own weapon so that she could back up Lucas.

"Nothing," Lucas said. "Where the hell are the men who are supposed to be protecting us?"

Kylie hadn't wanted to speculate, but she did anyway. And it wasn't good, either. She didn't know the guard or the deputies, but she doubted if all three were incompetent enough to miss tear gas canisters being noisily shot into the house. That meant the three men were likely incapacitated.

Or worse.

She heard the roar and hiss behind her, and she risked a backward glance. There were no longer just wisps of smoke, but a column of the black stuff rising through the attic opening. It was also coming in through the floorboards. The fire was moving fast and was no doubt already beneath them.

"Lucas?" she whispered.

He looked back at her, and even in the moonlight, Kylie saw his eyes widen.

"Get out of there now," he insisted.

She didn't need a second invitation. The smoke was already so thick that it was cutting her breath in two. Lucas held out his hand to help her, but she waved him off. "You keep watch. I can do this."

Kylie stepped onto the box and crawled through the porthole and onto the roof. She scrambled to position herself, not right next to Lucas, but in the opposite direction. At least this way, with two of them to return fire, they wouldn't be blindsided.

For what it was worth.

And it was worth only a few minutes at most because Kylie knew they couldn't stay on the roof.

She peered down at the front of the house and saw the orange-red flames lashing through what had once been the windows.

"How bad?" Lucas asked.

"Bad."

Lucas didn't waste any time. He used his foot to lower the chain ladder to the side of the house. The ladder clanged against the exterior. Probably alerting anyone and everyone. Not that they hadn't been alerted already. If the kidnappers had set the fire either intentionally or unintentionally with the gas canisters, they were no doubt watching and waiting for Lucas and her to attempt an escape. Hopefully, though, they wouldn't be looking in the direction of the roof.

"We go down together," Lucas instructed, "with me standing behind you so you won't be directly in the line of fire."

Despite her heartbeat pounding in her ears and the smoke clogging her lungs, she saw the flaws in that plan. Serious flaws. "Not a good idea. You'd have to hook your arms through the chain just to keep from falling. You'd have no way to defend yourself."

"But you and the baby would be protected."

Okay, there was another lump in her throat. More than a lump. It sent her heart soaring to know that he'd give up his life for the baby. But Kylie couldn't let Lucas's offer to protect her at all costs factor into this.

"If they start shooting, we both need to be able to return fire. Lucas, it's our only chance of all of us making it out of here alive, and you know it."

Kylie could see the debate going on in his eyes, but she knew that debate couldn't last long. Beneath them, the flames were roaring, churning out yet more suffocating smoke, flames and searing heat. It wouldn't be long before the entire house collapsed.

"Let's go," Lucas finally said. And he climbed onto the ladder. So that he was facing out. He hooked his left arm around the linked chains, so he could keep his balance, but his shooting hand was free.

Kylie followed him. Not slowly either. They moved quickly, both trying to keep a vigilant eye on their surroundings. Hard to do, though, when she couldn't see. The smoke was already too thick to get a good look at the yard or much of anything else.

With each step, Kylie wondered if it'd be her last, and she prayed. Mercy, did she ever pray.

Lucas stepped onto the ground and didn't waste a second. He took hold of her arm and got them moving. Fast. Not toward the pasture and the woods, though. With a firm grip on her wrist, he barreled out from the meager cover of the house and started toward the barn. It wasn't hard to find. There was a dim light on inside, and the milky yellow illumination cut through the blanket of smoke and the darkness.

They had gone only a few steps before a bullet whistled past their heads.

Chapter Eighteen

Lucas hooked his arm around Kylie's waist and shoved her to the ground.

And it wasn't a second too soon.

Another bullet smashed into the side of the house, in the exact spot where Kylie had just been standing. He didn't want to think of how close she'd come to being killed.

Putting himself between her and the line of fire, he dragged them to a row of shrubs and raised flower beds. It wasn't much protection against bullets, but it was better than standing out in the open.

Lucas did a quick check to make sure Kylie was all right. Her breathing was rough and fast, and there was a smear of dirt on her right cheek, but other than that, she appeared to be okay.

For now.

He knew that could change in the blink of an eye.

Lucas looked out through the shrubs and checked the grounds. Specifically, the area from where those shots had originated. And, thanks to the light from the fire, he quickly spotted the shadows behind a corral fence that was adjacent to the barn.

There were two men armed with rifles with scopes mounted on them.

And the figures weren't stationary, either. The men moved slowly, barely an inch with each step while shielding themselves behind the wooden fence. With each step, they got closer, and Lucas's heart pounded faster and harder, until he thought it might come out of his chest.

Lucas figured he could probably get off a shot if he left cover. Of course, that would leave Kylie in a highly vulnerable spot since the remaining gunman would no doubt turn that rifle on her.

Hell.

How had things come to this? Lucas couldn't take the time to berate himself, but he'd sure do it later. He should have insisted they leave the ranch while they had a chance. He should have pressed harder to find a safe house. Now, his mistake just might cost them their lives.

A chunk of the flaming roof tumbled to the ground, bringing with it more smoke and fire. Lucas waited, praying the smoke would soon clear because he needed to move Kylie.

They were much too close to the burning house.

For that matter, they were much too close to those gunmen.

Beside him, Kylie whispered something, but Lucas

wasn't able to hear what she said. A blast drowned her out. A bullet slammed into the ground right next to her head. And it hadn't come from either of the two riflemen. No, this shot had been fired from the general area of the storage shed.

So, there were three gunmen. At least. That didn't do much to steady his heart. He couldn't see the one near the storage shed, but he still had a view of the others. Kylie's and his only chance was to turn the odds in their favor.

"I'll take the one on the right," Kylie said as if reading his mind.

It was the only thing they could do—eliminate the riflemen—but still Lucas debated it. Though a debate was useless. Both Kylie and he knew what they had to do. It was their only chance.

"Stay down as much as you can," he ordered.

"Ditto," Kylie ordered in return.

They exchanged one last glance, and in that too-brief moment, a thousand things passed between them. Lucas wished he had time to tell her things he should have said. But there was no time. Kylie moved, levering herself up slightly so she'd have a better position.

Lucas did the same.

He took aim and squeezed the trigger. Beside him, Kylie did the same. One shot each. Thick, loud blasts that tore through the smoke and moonlight. And Lucas immediately ducked back down. Thank God, Kylie did, as well.

And he waited.

Listening.

"Two down," Kylie said. "One to go."

Only then did Lucas realize she'd lifted her head to look through the shrubs. Cursing, he pushed her back down, came up and fired. Not one round. But three. Finally, he saw the rifleman in the pasture collapse onto the ground.

There wasn't a second of reprieve. Definitely not even time to take a breath.

Above them, Lucas heard the groaning sound of the wood, and he saw what was left of the attic tear away from the frame of the house. It was coming down.

Right on them.

Lucas grabbed Kylie's arm, though she had already started to move as well. They launched themselves off the ground.

"The barn," Lucas shouted.

And he let go of her so he could take aim. Even though they'd taken out all the visible shooters, that didn't mean there weren't others. He knew there was still a risk of being shot, and that the person could easily do that while they were out in the open. However, it would have been an even greater risk for Kylie and him to remain by the shrubs.

The attic and a good portion of remaining roof crashed onto the flower beds and sent sparks and flames flying. Lucas didn't look back. Instead, Kylie and he raced toward the barn and ducked inside.

No shots.

Thank God.

But that didn't mean they were safe.

They'd barely stepped inside when Lucas heard something he didn't want to hear. There were the sounds of a struggle, and there was the smell of fear.

He pushed Kylie behind him again and saw what had caused those sounds.

It was Cordelia.

KYLIE BLINKED to make sure the smoke hadn't affected her vision. It hadn't. Cordelia was there in the barn. Standing with her back pressed against one of the stall gates.

Sweet merciful heaven, was she the person responsible for those gunmen?

If so, Kylie knew she didn't stand a chance of holding her temper because those three men had nearly gotten them killed.

"What are you doing here?" Lucas demanded, taking the question right out of Kylie's mouth.

But Cordelia didn't answer. She stood there, shivering. Trembling, actually, from head to toe. And it was only then that Kylie noticed she wasn't wearing a jacket. In fact, not even long sleeves. She stood there barefoot in only a pair of girlie pink silk lounging pajamas that were dotted with tiny flowers. Hardly the attire for a trek outside in January.

Or for an attack.

It was on the tip of Kylie's tongue to ask what had happened, but Kylie's question was delayed when Cordelia's eyes angled in the direction behind her.

Into the darkened stall.

Kylie and Lucas both aimed their weapons at the stall. And Kendrick Windham raised his head. Kylie saw Windham's hands covered with surgical gloves. And then she saw the gun. Not pointed at Lucas and her, but at Cordelia.

"He kidnapped me," Cordelia muttered, her voice ripe with fear.

"Guilty," Windham volunteered. "I'd so hoped it wouldn't come down to this." He sounded only mildly annoyed that he now had a hostage situation on his hands.

Kylie was annoyed, as well, but there was nothing *mild* about her reaction. They'd moved from one dangerous situation to another. Worse, neither Lucas nor she had a clean shot. If she fired now, she'd put Cordelia, and ultimately them, in even greater danger.

"Your hired guns are dead," Kylie gladly let him know. It also let him know that he was outnumbered. Of course, that didn't take away his advantage, not with his gun aimed at Cordelia.

"Hired guns? That's such a generous term for them. I'd prefer to call them idiots. All they had to do was kidnap you and bring you to me. But did they do that? No. They had to get Sheriff Creed here involved. The last person who should be involved in anything like this."

"Yeah. I see your point," Lucas interjected. Unlike Cordelia, there was no fear in his voice. But Kylie heard lots of determination. He wouldn't give up without a fight. "If your *idiots* hadn't botched the kidnapping, then you could have killed Kylie, and I would have never known about the illegal surrogacy activity. Or that she was carrying my baby."

"Oh, trust me, I would have come up with a reasonable substitute for a child. There's always a solution when money's involved. After all, I wouldn't have wanted to forfeit your final payment."

Money was his motive. Windham obviously wanted to silence her, and now Lucas, because they would have ultimately threatened his income.

"What did you do to the guard and the deputies?" Lucas demanded.

"They're alive. I used tranquilizer darts on them just like the ones I used on the dogs. Despite what you think of me, I don't enjoy killing. But I'll do it, if necessary. I think I proved that with Tiffany Smith."

"Among others," Lucas interjected.

"No others. Only Ms. Smith, who had a penchant for not keeping her mouth shut. Thankfully, she was one of a kind. My other surrogates are obedient and make me what I am—a very wealthy man. They'll continue to make me wealthy, too. Which is why we need to end this little encounter soon before those men you hired wake up from the sedation."

So, time was on their side. Maybe if the guard or one

of the deputies came out of the sedation earlier than Windham had anticipated, they'd call for backup. However, Kylie couldn't count on that happening.

"You're holding an innocent woman hostage," Kylie pointed out. Then, she paused. Rethought that. "Cordelia *is* innocent, isn't she?"

"Of course, I am!" Cordelia snapped. Gone was some of the fear, and in its place was more than a little anger. Kylie understood that anger.

Windham had put all of them in grave danger.

"Well, she's innocent only in a legal sense," Windham explained. "But the police will think differently. It's her gun, by the way. So, her fingerprints are already on it. I need a scapegoat, and that means I'll have to set her up to take the blame for all of this."

Cordelia's mouth tightened. "You what?" But asking that unnecessary question wasn't the only thing she did.

"Don't!" Lucas shouted.

Cordelia either didn't hear him or didn't heed his warning because she turned, apparently to launch herself at Kendrick Windham.

Windham was fast. And lethal. He repositioned his gun a few inches lower and pulled the trigger.

The bullet sliced through the outer edge of Cordelia's shoulder. Cordelia screamed, a bloodcurdling sound. But she didn't fall to the ground as Kylie had hoped she would. That would have given her a clear shot at Windham. Instead, Windham hooked his left arm around Cordelia and fastened her back against his chest.

A human shield.

Except this human shield was bleeding, moaning and cursing in pain.

Windham jammed the gun to Cordelia's head and stared at Kylie and Lucas. "Now that you know I mean business, drop your weapons. And I won't ask twice. The next bullet goes in her head."

This was being caught between a proverbial rock and a hard place. If they didn't put down their guns, Kylie had no doubts that Windham would kill Cordelia and then try to kill them. Of course, they'd be attempting to kill him, as well. Which meant bullets would be flying.

Someone would die.

And Kylie couldn't be sure that the someone would be Windham.

"Don't shoot her," Kylie said to Windham. Not that a request or even begging would help at this point. But she hoped to distract him long enough for either Lucas or her to do something. "It's obviously me that you want."

"What the hell are you doing?" Lucas demanded in a gruff whisper.

Windham paused, staring at her. "You're absolutely right."

Before the last syllable left his mouth, he fired a shot at Lucas. It missed.

Barely.

Lucas scrambled to take cover against one of the empty stalls. He yelled for Kylie to do the same. But

Kylie didn't have a chance. Windham shoved Cordelia straight at her. The impact rammed their bodies together, catching them off balance.

Kylie's gun clattered to the floor.

And before she could regain her balance, Windham reached for her. Kylie had one thought.

A horrible one.

She would die before she had the chance to tell Lucas that she was in love with him.

WINDHAM MOVED fast.

Too fast for Lucas to get off a safe shot or for Kylie to try to escape. The man seized Kylie's arm, and in the same motion he shoved the semiautomatic against the back of her head.

Lucas immediately aimed his weapon and stepped out from the cover of the stall. "Put down your gun, Windham, and let her go."

Lucas said the words by rote after years of having been a sheriff, but there was nothing rote about the fury that rose in his throat. Or the rock-hard knot that tightened in his stomach.

The SOB had Kylie.

Lucas met her gaze. For only a second. It was all he could handle, or it'd distract him at a time when he needed no more distractions. However, he couldn't completely dismiss that look he saw in Kylie's blue eyes. Fear, yes. But not as much as he'd expected to see there. She was doing her best to keep herself together.

"This won't help," Lucas said as calmly as he could manage. He glanced at Cordelia to make sure she wasn't bleeding profusely. Thankfully, she was lying on the floor and had managed to clamp her hand over her wound. But she still needed medical attention ASAP. "Surrender your weapon, and you won't be hurt. You've got my word on that."

"Your word. And that's supposed to make me feel reassured? Well, it doesn't. The only reassurance I want is a trip away from this place, and I want Ms. Monroe to come with me."

So he could kill her.

And that's why Lucas had to figure out how to end this now.

Windham kept stepping back, moving toward the back exit of the barn. Kylie's expression didn't change, but she no doubt knew where this scum was taking her. Her life wouldn't be worth a dime if he got her outside the line of fire. He'd simply kill her when he no longer needed a hostage to escape.

And worse, Lucas wasn't sure how long Kylie could keep up that cool veneer. If she panicked, Windham would likely kill her on the spot. In his experience, criminals didn't like noisy hostages.

"Tell me what it'll take to get you to release her," Lucas offered. He hoped it'd stop Windham from moving.

It didn't.

"Trade me for her," Lucas suggested. "I'm a sheriff.

The cops will be more than willing to bargain with you if you're holding me."

"You don't understand. I have no wish to bargain."

In other words, he wanted to carry out his plan of killing all of them.

That couldn't happen.

He couldn't lose Kylie and the baby. He just couldn't. And in that moment, he realized just how true that was. He only hoped he got the chance to tell her. Because he was about to do whatever it took, including sacrificing himself, to make sure she got out of this alive.

Lucas quit thinking, and he reacted out of instinct to protect Kylie and their baby. He lunged toward Windham, only to see Kylie slam her elbow into the man's stomach and tear away from him. She dove forward to the floor, grabbed her weapon and came up ready to fire.

Windham turned in her direction.

He also turned his gun on her.

Lucas's response was automatic. He aimed high and fast. For the head. Two shots. A double tap of gunfire. Shots not meant to distract or injure. Shots meant to kill.

The gun blasts ripped through the barn. Kylie didn't move. She kept her gun level, in case Lucas's shots hadn't done the job.

But they had.

Windham collapsed into a heap, his weapon dropping to the ground.

Lucas hurried to the man to make sure he was dead.

He was. The shots had done exactly what they had been intended to do.

"It's over?" Cordelia asked.

Lucas nodded and turned back to Kylie. She was pale and shaky, but other than that, she was fine. He couldn't say the same for himself. It might take him a dozen years or so to get over almost having lost her.

He made his way to her and pulled her into his arms.

Chapter Nineteen

Kylie came out of the kitchen and set the Blue Willow plate on the table. She had a fork in her hand and was ready to do some groveling.

Finn stared at the contents of the dish as if it were navel lint. "What is it?"

"Crow."

His eyebrow arched. "Crow?"

"Well, symbolically it's crow. Literally, it's blackened veggie beef with peppercorns that I've sorta shaped to look like a crow." Even Kylie had to admit it didn't look that appetizing.

"It looks more like a charcoal bunny," Lucas pointed out.

"Maybe. But let's all use our imagination and think crow." She turned to Finn. "That's why I called and asked you to drop by—so you could see me eat crow."

Finn glanced at Lucas, who just shrugged. "Hey, I just wanted to apologize for thinking you were a criminal. The crow was Kylie's idea."

Finn stabbed some of the "crow" with his fork and had Kylie sample it.

"Yuck." She managed to swallow it, and that seemed to be all the punishment he was willing to force on her. "I'm really sorry."

"Me, too," Lucas added.

Finn nodded, trying to appear to be his old cocky self, but Kylie thought he was a little sentimental about all of this. "Apologies accepted from both of you."

Probably so they wouldn't have to look at it, Lucas put the plate on the counter behind him, and he and Finn finished off the longneck bottles of beer. Kylie settled in for her evening with a glass of milk, which she'd spiked with gobs of malted chocolate syrup, her own version of a celebratory treat. And there was no mistaking that they were celebrating. Windham was dead, the illegal operation had been shut down, and a new clinic would soon open to serve the needs of those who wanted qualified, legitimate surrogates. Even more, they were alive. All was right with the world.

Well, almost.

"How are your dogs?" Lucas asked.

"They're back to their old sweet selves. Cordelia, too."

"Sweet?" Kylie challenged. She started to sit down in the empty chair next to Lucas, but he snared her and pulled her into his lap instead.

That earned them a little *hmm* sound from Finn.

"Cordelia is on the mend and is singing your and

Lucas's praises," Finn continued. "She's not using the s-word anymore. As in *sue*. She dropped the lawsuit. And she said she hoped you would forgive her for all the ugly things she said and did to you. I'm telling you—Cordelia's had a real change of heart,"

"I guess having someone save your life does that to you," Lucas concluded dryly. "Isaac Dupont doesn't seem so riled at us either."

"Probably because we cleared his name by nailing Kendrick Windham," Kylie pointed out. "According to Sgt. O'Malley, SAPD discovered that Windham had doctored all sorts of paperwork to make Dupont look guilty. I guess Windham did that to cover himself in case the clinic was investigated. If it hadn't been for that doctored paperwork, I would have never suspected Dupont, and I certainly wouldn't have *alluded* to him in the article I wrote."

Lucas circled his arm around her and put his hand on her belly.

Finn obviously didn't miss that, either. Both his eyebrows lifted. "I get the feeling I should go so you two can have some private time."

"We already had private time before you got here," Kylie teased.

But Finn got to his feet anyway and tossed his empty beer bottle in the recycling bin by the sink. He looked at them. "So, are you guys going to shack up here at Kylie's place?"

Lucas nodded. "Until I can rebuild the house."

And Kylie didn't mind if that took, oh, forever to do that. Still, she was probably looking at three months at most. In other words, Lucas would be in his new home about six weeks before he became a father.

The corner of Finn's mouth hitched. "You two really look like a couple."

"A couple of what?" Lucas joked.

"That's to be determined." Finn took his jacket from the back of the chair, slipped it on and then extracted a folded sheet of paper from his pocket. "Okay. Here's my way of tormenting you for temporarily believing I was a depraved kidnapper and killer."

"What is it?" Kylie asked suspiciously.

"I've written down the gender of your baby. And a name suggestion to go along with it. Since both of you have said you didn't want this information, then I'll just put it here on the table, where it can stay for the next four and a half months. Because I know you won't change your mind and peek."

Kylie and Lucas exchanged glances. "Oh, that's cruel," she let Finn know.

"My form of revenge." He kissed Kylie's cheek and gave Lucas a friendly jab on the arm. "Be happy, guys, because, heaven knows, you deserve it." He added a wave. "Don't get up. I'll see myself out."

Because Lucas's embrace was far more interesting than her chocolate milk or seeing Finn out, she set the glass on the counter next to the "crow" and snuggled against him. "You won't mind the gossip about us living here together?"

"Maybe I will. A little. I'm an old-fashioned kind of guy."

She turned on his lap, repositioning herself so that she faced him. "Old-fashioned guys don't have sofa sex."

"They do. Floor sex, too."

Kylie smiled. "Add car sex while listening to Bob Dylan, and you'll get me hot enough to skip the fore-play."

He touched his mouth to hers. "What if I don't want to skip the foreplay?"

"Even better."

In fact, a lot of things were suddenly better. Espe-cially the alignment of their bodies. Kylie was already calculating how quickly she could undress him.

But Lucas obviously had something else on his mind.

He cupped her face in both his hands. "When Wind-ham had that gun on you—"

Kylie pressed her fingers to his mouth. "You don't have to talk about that."

"But I do." He eased her fingers away and repeated it so it was no longer mumbled. "Because I want you to know what went through my mind, what I felt, what I realized. And what I realized was that I'd forgiven you—and me—for what happened to Marissa."

Kylie was afraid to say anything, afraid to move, afraid to breathe for fear he'd take those words back, Words that she had prayed she would hear him say.

"You've done so much for me," he continued, his

voice a little thin now. "You made the sacrifices, Kylie. Huge sacrifices. You were willing to leave your home, your life and child just to make me happy. You gave me everything. *Everything.* You healed me. You saved me. And during those moments when Windham had that gun aimed at you, I knew I couldn't lose you. Ever."

"The baby—"

"Not the baby," he interrupted. "*You.* Don't get me wrong, I love this baby. But in that moment, I realized I love you, too."

She teared up immediately.

"Sheesh, I made you cry." He hurried to wipe the tears from her cheeks.

"It's the pregnancy hormones."

He laughed, low and husky. "Somehow, I knew you were going to say that."

"Then, do you also know that I'm going to say I love you, too?"

Lucas swallowed and nodded. "I'd hoped you would."

"You don't have to hope. It's as real and as strong as our baby's kicks."

Another nod. "If I weren't a cowboy, I'd cry." Judging from the quiver in his voice, he was on the verge of it.

Kylie kissed him. It wasn't a simple peck, either. It was long and French. Exactly what she thought the moment required. Because she wanted to remember this moment for the rest of her life.

Lucas loved her.

She loved him.

And they were going to have a baby. She didn't have

a clue what she'd done to deserve this kind of happiness, but she was going to seize it and not let go. Ever.

That kiss left them breathless, and it left Kylie wanting more. A lot more. "So, would you like sex before or after dinner?" she asked.

"Both."

Kylie laughed. "I think I'm going to like having you for a housemate," she whispered.

"You'll like it even more having me for a husband."

And just like that, she teared up again. "Blasted hormones."

Once more, he wiped away the tears and let his fingers linger on her face. "Will you marry me, Kylie? Will you be my wife so we can raise our baby together?"

That didn't just produce tears, it took her breath away. "Absolutely. Will you marry me?"

"In a heartbeat."

The happiness flooded through her. The warmth seemed to fill all the dark, lonely places. There were also more tears. She hadn't ever remembered being happy enough to cry. So, was this what love was all about? And better yet, this was only the beginning.

Lucas stood, scooping her up in his arms, and headed toward the bedroom. But then he stopped. She soon saw what had captured his attention.

She eyed the note that Finn had left on the table. Lucas eyed it too, and then they eyed each other.

"Should we?" he asked at the same moment that she asked, "You want to?"

Kylie debated it. Lucas obviously did, as well, which

was exactly the kind of sweet torture that Finn wanted them to experience. Finally, Lucas groaned, and while balancing her in his arms, he snatched up the note. He plopped it onto her belly and let her have the honor of opening it.

They read it aloud together.

"You should name him Bob Dylan Creed."

"A boy," Lucas said. "We're having a son." Now, there were tears in his eyes, proving real cowboys did cry when the situation dictated. And this situation definitely dictated. "But we're not naming him that."

"The name's negotiable," Kylie assured him. And this time she was the one to wipe the tears from his eyes. "What's not negotiable is everything else. Getting married, having this baby, living happily ever after."

"Especially that," he assured her.

And to prove it, Lucas kissed her. Long and French didn't even begin to describe this as his mouth thoroughly claimed hers. Building the fire and need inside her.

When he was done, Kylie knew she'd been kissed by a man who truly loved her.

* * * * *

Look for UNEXPECTED FATHER, Delores Fossen's next riveting romantic suspense, coming in April 2006 only from Harlequin Intrigue!

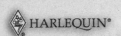
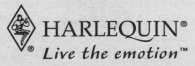

If you enjoyed what you just read,
then we've got an offer you can't resist!

Take 2 bestselling
love stories FREE!
Plus get a FREE surprise gift!

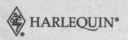